NO SPACE FOR JUSTICE

a novel

by

William N. Gilmore

William N. Gilmore

First printing (WhoooHooo!)

Book cover art & design by
Alex Storer
thelightdream.net

Book cover concept and co-designer
the talented and handsome
William N. Gilmore

ISBN: 978-1-946689-04-7

Manufactured by Kindle Direct Publishing
www.kdp.amazon.com

Printed in the (God bless the) United States of America

NO SPACE FOR JUSTICE

To Sharay!
Enjoy This Adventure
William N. Gilmore
APD

William N. Gilmore

Books You Really Need to Buy

by

William N. Gilmore

Books in the Larry Gillam and Sam Lovett

Detective Series:

Book One:

BLUE BLOODS & BLACK HEARTS

Book Two:

GOLD BADGES & DARK SOULS

Book Three:

BLUE KNIGHTS & WHITE LIES

***

Other Books:

***

Caution in the Wind

Book One: Partnerships

Coming Soon:

Book Two: The Treasure Seekers

***

Saints, Sinners, Lovers and Others

Poems and Prose

From Thoughts That Arose

Acknowledgements

Science fiction has always been my first love in reading. As a boy, I was inspired to write by the likes of Jules Verne with his stories of adventure to the Moon, gliding under the sea in a fantastic submarine, or racing around the world in a balloon. And H. G. Wells, who wrote about his fantastic machine traveling through time, invading Martians intent on our destruction, and a man standing right in front of you that you could not see.

I became enamored in the strange and wonderful stories. Meeting alien people like the ones on Edgar Rice Burroughs' Barsoom (Mars), and John Norman's barbaric world; Gor, or any of the other great SF writers whose stories I grew up with.

Some of my early attempts at writing science fiction were about UFOs, aliens, or robots; sometimes, all three in one. Science fiction might seem more exciting and a little easier than other stories to write when you're first starting out. Who's to tell you-you're wrong when you're drawing from your own imagination and making up strange worlds, space travel, aliens, and other things that seem impossible in the first place (at least for now?). Oh, and just for your information, George Lucas, a parsec is a measure of distance (about 3.26 light years, or nineteen trillion miles), NOT a measure of speed, but it's your story and it did pretty well. So, you are forgiven.

Now, after all these years, I finally wrote a full-length science fiction novel and had it published. So, thanks to all those science fiction writers before me who provided the inspiration. I hope I made you proud.

Maybe by reading this, another young reader will be inspired to open their mind and use their imagination in what is truly a grand adventure: writing.

*

I also want to thank all the members of the Paulding County Writers' Guild (pcwgga.org) for their help and support.

No, the apostrophe is not in the wrong place. The group is not possessive, but inclusive.

Please check out our website and if you are a writer, interested in writing, thought about writing, would like help becoming a writer, finding out how to put words together, or you would like someone to look over what you have written, whether you are a poet, a novelist, a songwriter, a playwright, or have just dreamed about it, come join us.

For my wife, Esther,

and all of our wonderful family.

William N. Gilmore

PART ONE

William N. Gilmore

CHAPTER 1

Exiting the Fulton County Courthouse, Detective Brian Douglas put on the felt fedora hat that was an adopted symbol of the Atlanta Police Homicide Squad. You received one when you solved your first murder case. All the detectives in homicide had earned them and for years they were respectfully referred to as "The Hat Squad" by fellow officers, the press, and many others. They were feared by the bad guys and for good reason; they were the very best.

He walked right into the cameras and microphones of a waiting swarm of anxious news reporters. Each of them yelling at the same time wanting him to answer their questions first.

Brian had not prepared anything to say, although he expected there would be a media frenzy after the verdict. It was common in such high-profile cases. Especially when it involved murder. And sex. And the fact that the defendant was an up and coming political figure, was just an added bonus.

The verdict was not a big surprise. The evidence was

sound, and Brian's testimony had sealed the deal. He was no rookie to murder investigations. He had been with the Atlanta Police Department for twenty-three years. Almost twenty of those had been with the Homicide Squad.

"Detective! Detective Douglas," a young, attractive reporter shouted. She held a large microphone with one of the local television station's logos on it. Her cameraman focused in on the two of them. Brian recognized her as the new reporter on the crime beat. "Are you surprised the jury took such a short time to reach a guilty verdict?"

Brian removed his dark-gray fedora, holding it in his hands. "Of course, not," Brian said smiling, making a connection with her by answering her first. "It was obvious from the start the bastard was guilty. I'm surprised it took them so long."

There were other shouts of questions, but Brian ignored them, wanting to continue with the young woman.

"Let me ask you something, Miss—"

"Jena Sparks, Channel Thirteen News."

"Well, Jena, what would you want if your, uh, sister was held as a sex slave for three days, tortured and sexually abused repeatedly until she died? That it was at the hands of a man who, because of his position, thought he could get away with it. On the other hand, as his defense, he said she had consented to the sex, given him drugs, and things got out of hand when she was the one who got too kinky. Then he tells you, without any remorse, that because it was her fault, he should not be held responsible. What would you want then, Ms. Sparks?"

The reporter swallowed hard and could not answer for a few seconds. "I'd want justice," she finally responded, falling into the trap to answer *his* question.

"Justice is for the civilized," he said, staring straight into her beautiful, blue eyes. "Justice is what people ask for in public, and in the courts, and we preach it to our children. However, I say revenge and punishment are in the minds and hearts of those who *really* want something done. Fortunately for this scum bag, I work for the so-called civilized society and didn't shoot him on sight. This judge, elected by the so-called civilized society, does not believe in the death penalty. Now, this so-called civilized society will have to house, feed, clothe, and care for this piece of trash for the next fifty or so years depending on the judge's sentence. And that will be at the civilized taxpayer's expense. The victim's family will repeatedly be reminded that this animal is still alive while they will never have their loved one back. Is that justice? Who's really getting punished?"

Detective Douglas scanned over the dozen or so reporters present. He nodded his head and continued.

"Most of you know me. You know my story and my record. You have been there with me for most of my cases. When there is a life snuffed out by another, I don't rest until I solve the case and make sure the person responsible is, as they say, brought to justice in court, or put in the ground. Don't you think it is time we took our civilized justice to them? Don't you think it is time we made sure criminals understand we will not just stand by and be victims at their leisure? I say make the criminals the victims. Put them on notice that from now on, we are the hunters and they are the prey. Take our fear and put it in their hearts. I say do unto others before they do it to you. However, it is your choice. You," he said pointing out into the crowd and then into the camera, "the so-called civilized society."

A few onlookers clapped. Even a few reporters were nodding their heads. The pretty reporter had an astonished look on her face. Brian wasn't sure if it was from what he said or the fact she was really getting all this recorded for the evening news lead story.

"Okay, folks," Brian said, placing the hat back on his head, "it's time for me to get off this soapbox. And no," he laughed, "I am not going to be running for any political office. Have a good day." He gave a wave and started down the courthouse steps. When he got near the street, he turned and looked back. She was gone. Not that he was interested in her. He was testing her. He wanted to check her resolve. He wondered if she was really cut out for this ugly business and where it led. He wondered if anyone really was—including himself.

What he did not see was the short, dark-suited figure watching him from the shadows across the street.

*

"Just what the hell did you think you were doing?" Captain Pealor, commander of the Homicide Squad, demanded. "Do you know that you've opened a can of worms that I can't close? I've been there to back you at some of your most vocal and, let's not forget, the less than stellar moments in your career. But this time, you just had to go and say your piece. And in front of reporters and TV cameras no less. In other words, in front of several hundred thousand people!"

"But I was just—"

"Don't say any more. This is beyond my control now. The Chief was demanding your badge, but by some miracle, I got him to agree to a ten-day suspension and additional training. The suspension starts now."

"Suspension? But I have cases. I've got—"

"Do you think you're the only homicide cop on the force? Maybe you do, but as of right now, you are a civilian. Give me your badge, your weapon, and your department ID. Go fishing, play some golf, build a birdhouse, or whatever it is you do. Relax, clear your head a bit, and get off that high horse you're on. You're too wound up. I bet you haven't had a vacation in years. Now, get out. Be back in ten days. And give all your open case files to Lieutenant Cummings to re-assign."

Detective, or rather, Mr. Douglas left the captain's office not bothering to stop at his desk to gather any files. Those were *his* cases, and no one was getting their hands on them. They were his to investigate and solve.

Brian stormed all the way down to the ground level parking lot where his car was located, threw open the door and climbed in. Bringing the car to life, he sped off the police parking lot, squealing his tires and sending up a gray cloud of dust and burnt rubber as he made the turn onto the street. He was not quite ready to head home. He was still steamed and needed time to cool off a bit. Maybe a lot of time.

If it had been thirteen years earlier, he might have stopped at the nearest liquor store and bought a bottle or two. That had been a rough time. He lost the love of his life, his beautiful wife, Angie. Turning to the liquid consolation during that time had almost cost him his job, and nearly his mind.

Surprisingly, it had been his job that may have saved him. He threw everything into it. Every spare minute. If not for any other reason except to keep his mind occupied with other things than thinking about the next drink. He was not just working on cases, he was solving cases. His intuitions and insights always seemed to work out. Asking the right questions and acting on his gut feelings helped to put many bad guys away.

With the support of his supervisor and the other detectives, he traded in the bottle and became a workaholic. In some ways, it made him who he was today. Maybe, the liquor would have been easier.

CHAPTER 2

Brian didn't play golf and he sure as hell didn't build birdhouses. However, he did do a little fishing. In fact, it was not widely known through the department, but he had a small cabin on one of the lakes on the Georgia-South Carolina state line.

To tell the truth, it wasn't really his but had belonged to his wife who inherited it from her grandfather. She had been the fisherman, or rather, the fisherwoman and re-introduced him to the sport he enjoyed in his youth. She placed it in her will with hopes he would use it if she went first, but since her death, he hadn't been to the cabin more than a dozen times. Some of those were just to make sure no one was shacking up in there and to keep it in usable condition.

He could not bring himself to sell it and never let anyone else use it. It provided some small connection to his wife. He was not about to share that.

He packed for a three to five-day stay and loaded up his truck with his casting rods and gear. He would stop at a store near the turnoff to the cabin and get additional supplies. He had made a list: including fuel oil for the eighty-year-old stove, matches, candles, bug spray, suntan lotion, bottled water, and a large pack of toilet paper among other essentials.

The two-hour drive was pleasant but lonely. The early fall weather was mild that morning when he left and warmed only slightly as the sun rose higher, shining in on the unoccupied passenger side.

It wasn't the same car. It couldn't be. It was another make and model, a newer year, it had different smells, and it looked so different, especially without her next to him.

In the past, there had been many a laugh from that side with stories and sights to share. Even some hand holding and playful groping. Now, it was a place to put his hat.

At the store, he snagged up the items on his list, making sure both large coolers in the back of the truck were filled with ice, as well as picking up a few other non-essentials, such as a large pack of cookies and a six-pack of cream sodas. He still had his weaknesses.

Getting to the cabin just before noon, Brian made sure everything was still secure and in good shape before unloading. Once, what now seems a lifetime ago, but with the memory fresh on his mind, he and Angie arrived at the cabin to find a broken window. A family of raccoons had taken up residence inside and they were not quite ready to leave at his request. He used a can of pepper spray he kept in the glove box to get rid of them. That little mistake forced Angie and him to sleep outside that night as well.

He remembered how Angie had laughed at him, but still

hugged him, calling him her hero. They both had a good laugh and later made love under the soft light of the moon. How he missed her touch, her smell, her face, and her sweet laugh.

Having settled in, Brian grabbed his casting rod and his tackle box before heading to the lake. He put his hat on, letting it sit far back on his head to keep the sun off his ears.

A small pier jutting out over the water was still standing although it didn't look like it would last but a few more seasons. He gingerly walked to the end, stepping over several of the spaces left by the missing or broken boards, and sat. He remembered sitting there at the end of that same pier with Angie, holding hands, her head on his shoulder, looking up at the night sky trying to spot satellites and shooting stars and pointing out the various constellations. Their favorite was Orion.

It seemed every spare thought was of her. It didn't matter where he was or what he was doing. You would think that over the years he would have moved on some, or at least, not let the memories affect him as strongly. However, this man was totally in love and devoted to one woman. He promised that devotion to her, not for the rest of her life, but for his. He would be true to that promise.

Brian had little luck. The fish just were not biting. Nevertheless, fishing was not always about catching something. He opened his tackle box to get a different lure. He spotted an old, used band-aid in one of the compartments. He took his hat off, placing it beside the tackle box and picked up the band-aid, examining it. It had small red hearts on the outside beige, plastic strip. He had wrapped it around Angie's finger after she accidentally hooked herself trying to release a small fish. She later took it off and put it in the tackle box. He smiled and placed it carefully back in the compartment.

After several hours, all he had done was throw back a few small sunfish and lost two jigs. It was now getting to be late afternoon, so he headed back to the cabin.

Brian was unaware of the large set of eyes watching him from across the lake, just as they had done all day.

*

It took him several tries to get a fire started in the old cast-iron stove, but he finally conquered the task. It would have been a chilly night without it. He was thankful he bought the fuel oil to help get it started.

He made a couple sandwiches and had chips to go along with his cream soda. He set up several candles and lit the modern hurricane lamp that stayed at the cabin. The cabin was just about as rustic as it could be. Although he had clean well water from the pump in the small kitchen, there was no electricity, no modern indoor plumbing, no phone, and best of all, no neighbors. At least no one close enough to hear. Angie wanted to keep it as original as when her grandfather first built it. That had been just fine with him. He didn't want to pour any money they didn't have back then into it.

The bedroom, which was actually part of the living room, if you could call it that, had the only modern piece of furniture. The bed had been Angie's idea. It had been big enough for both of them, barely. It was just right.

Brian put things away and shut down the cabin for the night. He had a single portable fluorescent light that he placed on a stand next to the bed, so he could read and munch on his cookies with another cream soda.

It wasn't long before he began having eye flutters and found himself reading the same passages several times. He surrendered to the obvious, closed the book, and turned off the lamp. As he lay there, he listened to the night songs of many different creatures, and as he always did before going to sleep, he said goodnight to his wife and gave her a kiss in the dark. He hoped the nightmares would stay away for just a while.

William N. Gilmore

CHAPTER 3

Something was wrong. Something screamed inside Brian to wake up. This was not one of his usual nightmares. Brian opened his eyes and saw a reddish light all around him. He thought the cabin was on fire. He immediately believed embers from the old stove's fire had jumped out and the fire somehow spread.

He tried to leap out of bed, but it was as if he had been tied down although there were no apparent ropes or straps. He could move his head and see all around but that was all. He tried to will his legs to bend and strained to reach out, but to no avail.

He wondered if someone was taking revenge on him. Had he been doped or poisoned? Very little scared him, but this was no ordinary situation.

Now close to panicking, he fought desperately against the invisible bonds holding him, believing he was fighting for his very life. He mustered all his strength for one great thrust, screaming through clinched teeth as he tried to get his body to overcome the phantom force, his muscles aching, burning, stretching to their limit. The attempt failed.

Exhausted, he tried calling out but didn't think anyone was there to hear him. Even if there was someone, it probably would only be the person who put him in this situation.

His physical efforts having failed, Brian resorted to the only thing left. He tried to reason with himself about the circumstances of his predicament. He fell back on all his years of training and experience. He took deep breaths, calming himself and taking control of his fear. He explored and reasoned what was going on around him. Some things didn't make sense.

The fire; it had no heat, and there was no smoke. There was no crackling sound of burning. Just the light, but it wasn't a fire, it was a glow. A steady glow that filled the inside of the cabin, but with no origin, no centralized point. It was getting so bright he had to close his eyes against the intensity.

Suddenly, Brian felt as if he were no longer alone. He could barely open his eyes. There was someone or something in the room. He wanted to shout out but found he couldn't speak.

The figure was now close to him. It blocked out some of the blinding, crimson light. A face, if you could call it that, bent down close to his. Brian desperately wanted to scream.

He felt a touch on his chest and heard a voice. He didn't so much hear it out loud as he felt it deep inside himself. The soft, comforting voice in his head simply gave him directives and positive assurance; "You are safe, be calm, relax, nothing will harm you, free your mind and body, you have no worries."

Brian suddenly felt a peaceful stillness. There were no problems, nothing hurtful or sad. He felt tranquil, weightless, as though he were floating while wrapped in a soft, warm light. He could see colors he had never seen before and knew things others never dreamed. He could fly and move through the universe at will just by using his mind.

Brian heard the angelic voice again. It gave him only one directive this time. The one-word command was so alluring, Brian could not resist. The voice's single word, "Sleep", had Brian immediately fall into a deep, dreamless slumber.

*

Brian awoke slowly. He had a hard time shaking out the cobwebs in his brain. His tongue was dry, and all his muscles ached. He thought for a minute he had fallen off the wagon and tied one on, but he hadn't taken any liquor with him to the cabin and none was stored there.

He suddenly noticed he was not in the bed he and Angie had shared. He was lying in a strange tube-like apparatus. The door of the thing was open. The next thing he noticed was that he was naked. He had no memory of what had occurred in the cabin other than falling asleep.

He sat up and found he was in a small, oval, sterile-smelling room with a soft reddish light that seemed to emanate from the walls and ceiling themselves. He looked around but saw there were no doors or windows.

What appeared to be a table was there and the only other thing in the room was a stand with what appeared to be clothing.

He got out of the tube, a little unsteady at first.

He didn't like being as exposed as he was and picked up the garments, which had the oddest feel to them. They weren't cloth and they weren't paper. He took a whiff of them, but they had no odor. He was not exactly sure how to put them on. Maybe putting them on was the wrong term. He found it was more like wrapping himself up in them. They stayed on without buttons or zippers and there was no need for sashes or tape. It was like giant contoured pieces of organic kitchen-plastic-wrap.

After Brian covered himself, almost kimono style, he cupped his hands at his mouth and yelled out to anyone who might be there. He quickly slammed his palms against his ears. The echo of his own voice nearly deafened him. He would not be trying that again.

He went to the wall and started searching for a hint of an opening. He went around the room several times, running his hands up and down, but still, he could not even find a crack.

There were no spaces between the floor and the wall, and the same with the ceiling and wall. It was as if the room had been poured into a one-piece mold. *Then how did I get in?* He wondered to himself. *Moreover, why am I here in the first place? And just where is here?*

He went over to the table or whatever it was and sat down. He was a little disoriented and lightheaded. *Surely, someone will come and check on me,* he thought. *Hopefully, feed me. Then, maybe someone could tell me what the hell is going on.* He almost yelled again. Almost.

After a few minutes, Brian began to feel a tingling sensation. The hair on his arms and legs pricked up. There seemed to be a hum in the air, but not quite distinguishable. A section of the far wall began to shimmer, becoming transparent. He was not sure if it was a hole or a window. He had never seen anything quite like that. Not even in a magic trick.

A flat, round platform came through the small opening that closed immediately after. It was not wheeled in, or pushed by some hand. It just seemed to float, and it stopped in front of him. It had some items on it that might be considered bowls. Some contained what looked like large fruit. Fruit that had to have come from the strangest trees or vines imaginable.

He bent down and sniffed the fruit things while keeping his eyes on the opening, just in case someone came in, or, he might have a chance to run out. Run to where, though, was a big question. And if so, from what?

He picked up one of the strange looking fruits and turned it over and over. He touched his tongue to it. As he did so, he was afraid that might have been a mistake. He was afraid it might taste bad, or even be poison. Then he reasoned, why would anyone go to all this trouble to poison him now? His hunger overtook his caution and he took a bite of the fruit. It was delicious. Not only was it the best fruit he ever tasted, it also quenched his thirst it was so juicy. He tried to determine what it tasted like most. Strawberries, bananas, raspberries, or peaches. All with sweet cream. There was just no way to describe it. He tried another and it was even better. Now, this was the way to poison someone.

Also on the tray was a bowl filled with a honey-colored liquid with a folded piece of fabric under it. It was not unlike what he was wearing. He put his finger in the bowl and then to his mouth. It had the consistency of water and no taste. He surmised it was to wash with and clean up after eating. When he finished, the hole reemerged and the tray went back out the opening and the wall became solid again.

Everything that had happened so far made him wonder even more about what strange place he might be in and if he was a prisoner, the subject of an experiment, having a bad dream, or if he had just gone stark raving bananas. He was sure he was not dreaming and that left other options of which he was not too fond.

Just as he begun to wish he had yelled out while there was an opening in the wall, he got that feeling again where the hairs on his arms and legs began to rise and he felt the hum inside his head. The wall opened again. It opened even larger than it had before. What came through the opening made him rethink the option of whether or not he had gone mad. What he saw put that at the very top of the list.

CHAPTER 4

Brian backed away as far as he could but kept his eyes on the creature before him. It had on garments similar to what he was wearing but in a different configuration. He referred to the creature in his mind as *it*, because *it* was definitely not human, and it didn't look like any animal he was familiar with, and he could not say with any certainty if *it* was male or female.

"Do not let my appearance startle you. I am not of your world. My name, as well as many of our words, are not pronounceable by your tongue, so you may refer to me as you wish. I am sure you have many questions and I will be happy to answer what I can. You are in no danger. You are here to help us. You were being kept safe in this chamber, otherwise, you would not have survived the journey."

Brian could not take his eyes off the figure. It was frightening and beautiful all at the same time.

Standing before him was a creature just barely five feet tall. The oversized head was triangular shaped with large, almond-shaped eyes, spaced wide at the top. Not much of a nose and just a small slit for a mouth. It had two thin arms and three legs, or maybe it was three arms and two legs, it was hard to tell, but the large hands and feet had ten long, spindly fingers or toes each. The entire body was iridescent.

There had been no outward voice. Everything he had heard was in his own head. He believed it was talking to him telepathically. That scared him even more. Were any of his own thoughts safe? Was his mind being probed without his knowledge? Could his thoughts be used against him? What was the journey that he could not have survived?

"Your human species has not learned to control their individual thoughts yet. You are not being probed. In fact, it is against our customs to enter someone else's thoughts without permission. You do not possess the ability yet to naturally block your mind and you are sending out all your thoughts as if they were a handful of wheat husks tossed into the air."

"How is it you are communicating with me in English?" Brian asked.

"We know many Earth languages. We have been observing and learning about your species for many of your Earth years. We have groups of observers all over your world. I was one, myself."

"You mean spies?"

"I mean students."

"Then why am I a prisoner here? Why am I on this journey you mentioned?"

"You are not a prisoner. As I have told you, we need your help. All will be made clear to you when we arrive at my world."

"Your world? You mean out there," he pointed up. "Then, we are on a ship? A spaceship?"

"Yes, and we will be arriving very soon."

*

Very soon turned out to be about two days based on his sleep cycles and hunger pains just before meals of the delicious fruit were served. During that time, he had no further encounter with the creature he decided to call Jack, or with anyone or anything else for that matter.

The next thing he knew, he was being ushered out of his room by two Jack-looking creatures but somehow, he could tell neither was Jack. As he was taken out of the spaceship, and onto a docking platform, he found he was very light on his feet. Obviously, there was less gravity.

He got his first view of a strange, alien world. The air smelled sweet and the light from the red sun gave everything a soft rose-colored hue. He could not see very much of what was beyond the great structure before him. It was a massive thing. He was taken into a great hall through another strange portal. There he was placed before a group of Jack-looking creatures. He wondered how they could tell each other apart. He almost laughed thinking "he didn't know Jack".

All of a sudden, he had the worst headache of his life. He grabbed both sides of his head and would have dropped to his knees, but was caught just before he hit. The pain subsided immediately and he looked over at his rescuer. It was Jack. He thought it was anyway. He straightened and looked down at the creature.

"Is that you, Jack?" Brian asked.

"Yes. Why the name, Jack?" Brian heard the thought inside his mind.

"You popped into the room through the wall. It was like a child's wind-up toy. A Jack-in-the-box. It's all I could come up with at the time."

"They apologize for the bombardment of thoughts directed at you. They did not understand you had not received training. I have told them before how inferior your species' brains are and how you still retain only verbal speech. I will act as your go-between."

"Inferior? We are the dominant species on our planet," Brian said, looking back at the other Jacks. "We have spaceflight too. We have been to our moon. We've sent spacecraft to other worlds and far out into the universe."

"Yes, we all know," Jack said. Brian saw many of the others nodding their triangular heads.

Then a new, strong, singular voice resonated in his head. "We did not know if your species would ever be a threat in the universe to us, or any other civilization. We found you were more of a threat to yourselves. That is why we have been studying you since the dawn of your species. Our world, our culture, is many, many millions of years older and wiser than yours was. We have no wars, no sickness, and no poverty. There is no greed. There is no hate. We have no crime."

"That is the Guardian of The People," Jack said. He is the spokesman for our world and leader of the High Council."

Brian shook his head. "I hate to tell you this, guys, but someone sure fooled all of you. Just between you, me, and the disappearing doors, kidnapping is a crime. I was brought here against my will and *that,* sir, is a crime! I demand to be taken back to my world, good old Earth, right now!"

Again, the Guardian of The People sent his thoughts directly to Brian. "You have been brought here, at the direction of myself and the Council—for a purpose. However, we are afraid your world, the Earth you knew before you left, no longer exists. Therefore, we did not kidnap you as you say. We rescued you. We saved you."

Brian recoiled a step. It was a while before he spoke.

"What do you mean Earth no longer exists? What did you do?" Brian asked. His eyes wide and a tear beginning to run down his cheek. "Did you destroy the Earth? Did you shoot some death ray at it or suck the air away from it? What did you do? I want to know, right now!"

"No, Brian," Jack looked up at him. "We did not destroy the world you knew. Your own people did. Over three hundred years after you and I left the Earth."

William N. Gilmore

CHAPTER 5

Brian was visibly shaken. Tears streamed down his face. Jack took him out of the chamber and into a private area.

"What destroyed my world? Was it war?" Brian asked somberly.

"No. Human's greed and failure to consider the consequences of their actions made the planet uninhabitable. They polluted the air and the water beyond their ability to repair it. They tried going underground. They even tried going to other planets. Time ran out. Almost everything died."

"You said my world was destroyed three hundred years after we left? It was only a couple of days. I hardly have any stubble on my face. That can't be right. This can't be happening." Brian questioned the reality of what he was told. He didn't want to believe it to be true.

"We are very far from Earth. The journey from your world takes many of your lifetimes. The pod you were in protected you, and you were not awake for the long journey."

"Then what about you? Why didn't you age?"

"But I did when I was not in my own stasis pod during certain dangerous parts of the journey. Not as quickly as you might have aged. Our lives are nearly endless. Some of our

35

elders were alive before your ancestral species walked your planet. I myself saw the building of your great pyramids on my first study of your civilization."

"But you are so advanced. Obviously, you have faster than light travel. What about time travel," Brian begged. "Things can be made right again."

"We have what you would call faster than light capabilities. We also use systems that you may know by the names, wormhole and black hole. Our scientists have developed some promising experiments using multiple black holes, but they have not perfected the manipulation of time. They have had only limited success."

"Do you mean I'm the last human alive?"

"No. There are others. We have saved many hundreds who would have been doomed by your natural disasters and catastrophic circumstances, not of their own making. Most are in stasis awaiting the day they can return to the Earth, one day when it may rejuvenate itself. Some are useful to us now and have positions in our society. But still, they are human and have human tendencies. Violence for one. That is where you come in. We need to go back before the Council. They will give you the details. Are you ready?"

"Yes. It's just a lot to think about," he said, wiping his eyes.

Brian went back into the chamber beside Jack. Jack was

making some motions with his hands. Obviously talking to the Council of Jack look-alikes. Brian could not hear him this time. It must have been a closed circuit. He wondered if, maybe, a few of the Council were reading his mind right then, even without permission.

Jack turned and looked up at Brian. "The Council requests your help and expertise in a delicate matter. A matter that has not risen in many thousands of years and has all the Council bewildered and on edge."

"So, now you're *asking* me to help you? You didn't bother to *ask* while I was still on Earth, while there still *was* an Earth. Now, I have no home to go back to and everyone I've ever known is dead and dust. I was kidnapped and brought before this so called highly advanced civilization where you don't even have any police, not a jail in sight, and now you try to tell me you have no crime? That's a laugh. I can't wait to hear why I'm so important to you that you've destroyed my life."

"Brian," Jack began. "The Council is asking, I am asking, for you to use all of your knowledge, all of your training, experience, and skills to help us solve a horrible crime."

"What happened? Did someone steal one of your spaceships and go for a joy ride around Orion's belt or did someone read a dirty thought they shouldn't have?"

"No, Brian," Jack stated. "This is much more serious. This is something that has not happened on our world for many of your Earth years. Something the Council has no knowledge how to investigate, how to obtain the truth, or what to do next. The Council is asking you to help us. Someone has taken a life."

Brian had been asked, by highly advanced creatures on an incredibly distant, alien world, a world without police, crime, or even a justice system, to solve the most heinous of crimes; murder.

CHAPTER 6

"Okay, let me get this straight," Brian began. "There is no body. There is no crime scene. There is no forensic evidence, no weapon, and no suspects. Does that about cover it?"

"That is correct," Jack sent to Brian.

"And when did this occur?"

"About eight hundred of your Earth years ago."

"Well, of course, it did!" Brian slapped himself on the forehead with the palm of his hand. "I should have guessed. I thought it was only a hundred years. How foolish could I have been? Case solved. He died of boredom. No. No, wait. I have it now. He was killed in the conservatory by Mrs. Peacock with the candlestick holder, or maybe, the butler did it."

Brian suddenly grabbed both sides of his head. The intense pain lasted just a second or two.

Jack looked up at him and Brian could almost swear the little slit of a mouth was turned up into a smile.

"I just wanted to clear your mind for you, so we can begin the work. I have been instructed by the Council to assist you with whatever you might need."

"I need a whole bottle of aspirin for this massive headache you gave me," Brian said, shaking his head.

Jack reached one of his long arms up and placed two of its ten fingers at the base of Brian's neck. All the pain flowed out of his head. In fact, it gave him a slight but pleasant buzz.

"What other little secrets do you have?"

Jack did not answer that question, but instead sent, "We should see the High Scribe at the archives center."

"Okay. You lead the way. I'm new here."

In just a couple of seconds, a circular flying vehicle appeared. It was like the one that brought him food on the ship, only much larger.

"This way," Jack instructed, getting onto the platform of the craft. It was only about five feet across and there were no visible controls, seats, or even any handholds. When he stepped onto the platform, he got that tingling feeling just like when the portal opened in his room on the spaceship. It began moving and gained speed, but Brain had no sensation of the movement. There was not even any wind in his face.

They traveled over and around and even through structures the likes of which Brian had never seen or ever imagined. He could see that parts of the beautiful city were domed as if they were in a huge see-through cake box. Long roads and high bridges used by strange vehicles connected parts of the city together.

There were fountains of rainbow-colored liquid rushing upward that suddenly transformed into solid shapes that danced and then abruptly burst like fireworks only to become liquid again.

Also, he saw simmering, three-dimensional figures of what looked like colored glass and metal swirling around each other, melting into entirely new shapes of impossible complexity.

Brian saw other flying crafts and occasionally he would see one with a human on it. There did not appear to be any traffic pattern and he never witnessed any close calls or narrow escapes. Even the humans he saw did not seem to be fazed by all that was transpiring around them.

The craft he was on came to a stop at a structure. It looked more like a huge, gold and glass church or cathedral.

"This is one of our oldest structures," Jack advised. "It holds the records of our history. Much like all of your Earth libraries and museums combined."

"I understand. Nevertheless, you mentioned a High Scribe. I guess that's similar to the head librarian?"

"It would be like a priest or a shaman, but so much more. He is an elder who also sits on the Council. He is revered and little is approved without his say."

"Ah, politics. The same anywhere in the universe. Grab the power and never let it go. Totalitarianism at its finest. And he is going to help us how?"

"There may be information stored here you could use to solve the case."

"Solve the case? I don't have a case. I don't even know if there was a case to begin with. I have nothing. Zero. Zilch. I don't even have eight-hundred-year-old dust."

"Please, wait until we have met with the High Scribe. What he has to show you may change your preconceptions of the task before you."

They entered the structure through another one of those disappearing doors Brian was so fascinated with and were met by another Jack-type person, but this one was visibly older. Much older. Moreover, he did not walk on two or three of his legs. He floated about the normal height for his species on a smaller version of the craft on which they just arrived. Two of his appendages were visible. The others, if they even worked at his advanced age, appeared to be covered.

Jack bowed to the High Scribe. Brian, taking his cue from Jack, also bowed.

Brian tried to think of something totally off the wall so that his mind was not open to the High Scribe.

"No, Detective Douglas, you are not in Kansas anymore." It was a new voice in his head. It had to be the High Scribe, Brian thought. "And I am not a wizard." The voice was clear and strong. For a moment, Brian thought for sure the High Scribe had spoken out loud.

"Too many of your early species have their thoughts consumed with violence, superstition, reproduction, or hunger.

Your mind is open, and your clear reception of our thoughts is rare among your people. Which is another reason you were chosen."

"Chosen?" Brian questioned. "I thought I was brought here to solve a murder. How was I chosen? And by whom?"

"It was I," came the response from Jack. "I had been watching you for some time before you were selected. I had other candidates, but they proved to be unsuitable for our needs. Your skills, the ability to adapt, and your capability to receive our thoughts were just a few of the factors considered. Your mind was like a clear beacon for me to locate among all the thoughts that were muddled in a sea of noise.

"I don't know if I should be honored or appalled that I was being spied on and my privacy was trampled. How long did you watch me?"

"I studied you for about twenty of your years," came Jack's thoughts. "I had already studied about forty of your people. Some were many years before your birth. I am embarrassed to report I wasted several of your years before I came to understand your civilization's concept of play-acting. That is something strange to us."

"You mean you don't have actors, people who pretend or disguise themselves for entertainment?" Brian was bewildered at this.

"No. We entertain ourselves in many other ways. On

your world, I would use my thoughts to have humans see me as something else. That would not be possible on my world."

"Wow! You would be fun at parties." Brian laughed.

Jack turned to face the High Scribe. There appeared to be an exchange between them. Brian saw Jack nod his head and bow again. He then turned to Brian.

"We will be taken to another section where we are hoping you will be able to receive the information from our archives. It will be very important you clear your mind and stay focused. The High Scribe will be your guide through this period. It is critical you follow his commands and not let your mind wander."

"Alright. Is there any danger? You're not talking about scrambling my brains, are you?" Brian gave a weak smile. He thought he was only half kidding.

"Several attempts have been made with your species to receive information from the archives, but most of the subjects had to undergo extensive rehabilitation. We are confident we will be able to utilize the information from those attempts, and, through your proven abilities, we believe success is attainable.

"That's just great. You're going to turn me into a zombie, or a drooling idiot." Brian gave a small chuckle, "I guess that is redundant. If you do, who will you get to solve your dusty little murder? Oh, that's right. There is no one on Earth to go back to get. Looks like you better take really good care of me. I am the chosen one."

"Yes, we will take care of you. We do not want to have to take you and put you on the planet of zombies." The thought had come from the High Scribe himself.

Brian's eyes got big and his mouth remained open for a few seconds before he finally spoke. "There's a planet of zombies?"

"Of course, not." The High Scribe returned. "It was just my attempt at human humor."

Brian couldn't help but laugh. It was more of what the High Scribe said about his attempt at humor that sent him into giggles.

"If you were not sitting on your little flying machine there, you would make a great stand-up comic."

That did not get any response from either Jack or the High Scribe.

William N. Gilmore

CHAPTER 7

Brian was on a table not unlike the one on Jack's ship, lying next to the floating High Scribe. He was given instructions and told what to expect so he would be comfortable with the session. He suddenly found his mind connected with the High Scribe. It was not just a voice in his brain, but a connection that went beyond the body. It was as if the High Scribe was walking him down a path. With every step, the scenery became clearer and the landscape continued to grow. Structures began to rise in the distance and soon he was among them.

The High Scribe was telling him things about the city and the world around them. Telling him in a voice, he could actually hear. The voice was familiar. One he had not heard in many years. The High Scribe pointed out and described the buildings and their uses.

He continued to guide Brian through a maze of structures that towered high above them and disappeared well below the level on which they were traveling. There were beautiful overhead bridges connecting many of the buildings. There were fountains, like the one he saw when he first arrived. Ruby-colored, crystal spires, thousands of feet, if not miles, high, appeared to be collecting the sun's rays, possibly turning them into useful energy conduits. He saw hundreds of the flying disks going in many directions, never in any danger of crashing into anything.

As they continued, the High Scribe directed him to a building just ahead. They made an entrance through the disappearing door system and Brian found himself in what appeared to be someone's living quarters.

"Does someone live here?' Brian asked the High Scribe.

"Open your mind. Look with your ability to see without your eyes. You did it on the journey here. What do you observe?"

Brian focused his thoughts. He could feel something outside his body. He could see the room without opening his eyes. It became clearer. He could see the room and he could smell the room. However, the room changed from what he believed he had seen with his eyes when they first entered it. There was something on the floor that did not belong. There was a smell that did not belong.

Brian sensed a form on the floor before he saw it in his mind's eye. He went over to it. It was a body. The murder victim. It was the body of a young, human female.

Brian wasn't sure how he was seeing this. An eight hundred-year-old crime scene complete with a body, and blood. He could even smell the metallic odor of the blood that pooled around the head as she lay on her right side.

"You may examine the body if you wish," interjected the High Scribe. "But you must push your mind deeper, control your thoughts to a degree you have never imagined, to be able to interact with what is before you now."

Brian knelt beside the girl and attempted to touch her shoulder. His hand felt a slight resistance as it passed through without making solid contact with her.

"Concentrate! Do not just do something without thinking about what it is you are doing. What it is you want to do. You must extend your thoughts as if they were your fingers. Touching your surroundings with your mind. Focus. Narrow your mind to your one objective."

Brian's body was shaking on the table beside the High Scribe. Sweat was pouring down the sides of his reddened face. His teeth were clamped together and the veins in his neck were bulging. There was a slight trickle of blood from his nose running down his cheek.

Again, Brian tried to touch the girl. His fingers felt the cold, dead skin for an instant. He moved her slightly and then his hand again slipped through and contact was lost.

He was exhausted. His head throbbed. His concentration was lost. He opened his eyes to find he was back in the room with the High Scribe and Jack.

"Good, very good," the High Scribe was hovering just above him on his personal little flying saucer. I did not expect so much from you this first time. You show much promise."

"Thank you, but tell me, just what the hell was that? How could we go back eight hundred years and see that?"

"Because it is still there. It is within a memory stored in our archives. We entered and became a part of that memory. With my help, you used your ability to interact with that memory. As your mind becomes more aware of its capabilities, expands its boundaries most of your species has either forgotten or suppressed, you will be able to control and use your thoughts in ways you have never imagined."

Brian started to get off the table, but the pounding headache was still there and he was very lightheaded. Jack came over and put the magic touch to the back of Brian's neck. He handed him a damp cloth to wipe his face. With the pain gone, Brian stood and asked if he might have something to drink.

"Of course," the High Scribe returned. "I believe you also require some nourishment now, and after, some rest. We have arranged for you to stay here so that you will have access to the archives as you wish."

Jack bowed, and Brian did the same as the High Scribe floated out of the room.

*

Jack took Brian to a large room where bowls of the delicious fruit had already been delivered for his refreshment. There was a bed. A comfortable bed and there was a rack with other garments on it.

Brian offered some of the fruit to Jack, but he declined. As Brian ate and drank of the fruit, Jack gave him instructions for use of objects within the room. Things were made simple for him since he did not have the ability to control objects with his mind. Illumination was manipulated with a sliding bar, attached to the wall, controlling the intensity. Another one controlled the temperature. A separate room was designated the hygiene room containing the facilities a human might need for cleaning. It was efficient and straightforward. Everything was one color. It was not a room you would want to spend a lot of your time.

"It's a little bland, don't you think?" Brian asked. "There's no kitchen, no television; there aren't even any windows. What about pictures or vases of flowers? Something to give it a comfortable, homey look."

"We do not have the need for the comfort of the likes humans relish."

"There is much I want to learn about you, your people, and your world," Brian said as he put the fruit he was enjoying back into a bowl. "I have—so many—questions. I have—I have to go to sleep now." Brian stumbled towards the bed, falling onto it just as he got there. He was asleep immediately.

William N. Gilmore

CHAPTER 8

Brian awoke refreshed, alert, and feeling very good except he was very hungry. He had no concept of time. He didn't know if it was day or night. He didn't know if this world even had a separate day and night. He went into the hygiene room and was glad he had received instructions from Jack on how to use the facilities. Otherwise, it would have been very embarrassing. There was no running water, just bowls of liquid. Everything, including shaving, used a process of ultrahigh sound waves.

When he came out of the room, he put on the new garments that were on the rack. That was something else Jack helped him correct. It seems he put the garments on incorrectly. In fact, he put them on somewhat—backward.

He found there was a fresh bowl of fruit available. He wondered if there was any other kind of food on this planet. A nice stack of pancakes and a cold glass of milk would be nice occasionally, not to mention, a good steak and a baked potato.

In addition, he was sure he had enjoyed his last bottle of cream soda. He became a little melancholy thinking of the lost material things of Earth, and then, a little angry with himself for being so selfish, thinking secondly of all the people lost. Almost all of humanity. Man's own fault.

Jack was outside asking if he may enter.

"Of course, come in." The portal opened, and Jack came into the room, "I don't guess there's a doorbell out there. Tell me though, if I wanted to go out, how do I open the portal?"

"That will come in time, but there is nowhere you would need to go. For your safety and to prevent confusion, it would be best for you to remain here unless escorted. Most of your time will be spent with the High Scribe or myself."

"Yes, I know we have much to do and I have a lot to learn, but I have so many questions. I want to see more of your world. I want—to—meet—others—I need—to meet with the High Scribe, now.

Brian found himself before the High Scribe. He was just a little confused about how he got there. So many things were strange, and he had many questions, but he knew there were important things for them to accomplish. He wanted to learn as much as he could about the process that allowed him to see eight hundred years into the past, and actually be a physical part of it.

He needed to learn more about the girl. Who she was and how she came to be on this world, and, how she lived her life and lost her life at such a young age so far from her home.

The High Scribe greeted him and Brian bowed. Jack was not present.

"I know you have many questions. You would not understand many things. They would require answers that would be meaningless to you. You must allow us to slowly teach you how to become aware of certain ways. It is not so much as being taught, as it is allowing your mind to awake to its full potential. You will find, with guidance at first, new and exciting abilities that have been hidden inside you. Nevertheless, beware. These abilities must be limited until your mind is strong enough, so you do not do permanent damage to yourself. More importantly, there is the possibility of damaging another. Until we are confident the danger is minimal, we are restricting your movements to your room and the archives."

"I understand," Brian said. "None the less, there are things about your world and your society I will need to know to assist me in my investigation."

"The one you call Jack will assist you with your requests. There will not be any other contact from any of our inhabitants. We ask you not to make contact with anyone of your own species."

"Is there any of my species who have the abilities such as yourself?"

"Some have learned to use limited abilities such as communicating, opening the portals, and controlling the crafts. However, attempts to go further in their teachings did not produce positive results. You show promise to go far beyond anything we have experimented with so far. Now it is time for us to revisit what you call the crime scene."

*

Brian was once again laying on the table with the High Scribe floating over him. He closed his eyes and concentrated. He pushed everything out of his mind and focused. His thoughts were of the girl. Her hair partially covering her face. The blood on the floor. The room where she was lying. Suddenly, he was standing beside the High Scribe. They had not needed to make the journey through the city to the building. Before it had been a stepping stone. A learning adventure. Now, he stood right in the room with the body of the young girl on the floor.

"Good," the High Scribe's thoughts were very clear. "You remembered the path to get here. You bypassed obstacles and circumvented time and brought us right to where you needed to be. You did that on your own. Impressive. Continue."

Brian knelt again beside the girl as he had on the previous visit. This time he suppressed the thought of her as being an eight-hundred-year-old corpse. He didn't think about how none of them were truly there. Or, were they? He would treat her as if she were his latest crime victim back on Earth, and this was a real crime scene. In fact, it was a real crime scene.

He focused on her for a few seconds and with a renewed confidence, touched her shoulder, making solid contact. Pushing on her shoulder while he held her head, he gently turned her on her back. He reached down and brushed the black hair out of her face. She was Asian. Maybe Chinese. Possibly even Mongolian.

No older than eighteen to twenty. He did not see any other wounds or bruises on her face or body other than the head wound. He examined her hands and did not see any defensive wounds.

"Does her body tell you anything?" the High Scribe was asking.

"It tells me many things, but I've learned over many years and through many mistakes, not to jump to conclusions." Brian ran his hands through the girl's hair and felt the back of her head where it was obvious something solid had struck her, opening her scalp and crushing the base of her skull close to where it connected with the vertebrate. He believed she had died instantly. Although he was not a coroner and had no medical training, his years as a homicide detective gave him some special insight. The damage to the girl's head revealed some clues.

Brian stood and surveyed the room. He walked around and looked all over. Up and down. It took him about ten minutes and the High Scribe did not disturb him.

Finally, Brian spoke. "I believe the girl was killed here. She died immediately from a single blow to the back of her head by an unknown object. That object was removed from the room."

"Do you believe this information will help you identify the human responsible for this act?" the High Scribe questioned.

"That and at least one other thing that may help to narrow down my search." Brian returned.

"And what would that be?" the High Scribe waited for Brian's answer, not invading his thoughts.

"That the suspect may not be human after all," Brian revealed.

CHAPTER 9

Brian suddenly found himself back in the room at the archives with the High Scribe. The High Scribe's thoughts were stronger, bolder than ever before.

"It is impossible any of our species could be involved. The diseases the human species carries; hate, greed, violence, deceit, and subversion, just to name a few, were eliminated from my world many thousands of your Earth years ago. Any offspring showing even the slightest tendencies of these diseases within its genes is discarded."

Brian was still a little shaky from his last session at the crime scene. The sudden return left him slightly dazed, but his recovery was quicker than before. His head hurt just a little, but not so much he couldn't respond to the High Scribe's rant.

"I let the evidence take me where it leads. There is still a lot to uncover. I can't say what happened yet, nor can I say with any certainty who may have been involved. I agree we humans are aggressive and self-centered. Those are characteristics of our species. Not diseases. You say your species was like that once itself. Maybe without those traits, neither of us would have survived to get where we are today."

"That may be true," the High Scribe rebutted, "but where

is your species today? That is right. They are dust on a barren world. Except for those who were saved and brought to this world. That was one of the few times I was overruled. The Council now sees I was correct after all. We must rid ourselves of the disease before it takes root again."

"You are wrong. I can see and feel the anger and the hate within you. The prejudice you carry may be suppressed among your own people, but you are sure to use it to your advantage when it comes to mine."

The High Scribe gave just the slightest physical hint of a reaction to Brian's reply. It was so subtle, Brian wasn't sure if he had seen it at all. Brian felt the High Scribe just on the edge of his thoughts. It was as if the High Scribe was looking into the window of his brain, but Brian was holding down the blinds. He had to focus intensely to keep the blinds from rolling up. There were things he learned he was not ready to share. He was starting to lose the battle.

Just then, Jack came into the room and he could feel the High Scribe backing off. His mental presence was no longer attempting to peer where it did not belong.

Jack asked if the session had been successful.

"Yes," Brian answered looking at Jack. "But I feel I could use rest again."

Jack looked at Brian. Again, Brian thought Jack's little slit of a mouth had, for an instant, turned up into a smile.

"What are you looking at, you wide-eyed, alien Jack-in-the-box," Brian asked with a jest at the otherworldly creature. "You, Brian. You are communicating without using your mouth."

*

Brian and Jack returned to Brian's quarters. Brian was surprised to find works of art on the now colored walls and stands with vases of strange and beautiful flowers. Brian sat on the bed as Jack rested back on his three legs.

"Thank you for decorating. I like the new couch and tables. Where did you come up with the art?"

"Some of the humans take up their time making these. I only wish for you to be comfortable. It may help in accepting your relocation."

"So, now you can read what I am thinking. I thought you weren't allowed to read my thoughts without my permission."

I am not reading your thoughts. You are sending me your thoughts. The ones you want me to read. It is the communication part of your thoughts that have developed quickly. You are now able to use them to some degree. Practice and development will be very important. However, it is not just what you send. It is also what you do not wish to send. You must also be able to block access to thoughts. And you must learn to do both at the same time."

"I've already had some practical application in blocking

an intrusive probe. It seems your High Scribe is not willing to abide by your own rules with regards to privacy. He tried to force his way into my thoughts after we had a disagreement on social issues."

"The High Scribe, because of his position, has the consent of the Council to act accordingly in the affairs of humans. Humans are considered inferior and even dangerous without regular monitoring. At least, that is what he has argued many times before the Council. The Council consented to him having this authority before the first human was brought to this world."

"How was I able to block the probe of the great and powerful High Scribe?"

"We did it together. Nevertheless, you responded with the training I gave you and you did very well."

"What training?" Brian questioned, showing his bewilderment. "I don't recall you giving me any training to block my thoughts."

"No. You would not. It was while you were asleep. Your subconscious abilities are strongest when there are no distractions. After your first session with the High Scribe, and seeing how advanced your abilities were, I decided it would be best if I were to assist you with your advancement of those abilities. For several of your days, while you slept and rejuvenated, I assisted you in your development."

"I slept for several days?" Brian exclaimed. "No wonder I was so hungry when I woke up. And you were here with me the entire time? Inside my mind?"

"Yes. Time is different for us." Jack explained. "We do not need the reoccurring rest periods humans need. In fact, our world, which is about ten times larger than your Earth, rotates at a much slower rate. That is why you do not feel the gravitational pull as you would on Earth. It takes three of your days on Earth to equal one of our world's rotations. Our sun, which is referred to by your scientists as a red giant, has a unique property that combines with the planet and gives us our long lives and our abilities. It has already started to affect you as well. Do not worry. It is not harmful."

"What exactly will I be able to do? Brian asked. "How far will your training go?"

"I can only influence your mind so far. You will be the controller. However, you must remember that you have the ability to cause great harm to yourself and to others, even without intent. You must check your emotions, and neither let them give away your thoughts nor allow them to rule your thoughts."

"That's easy for you to say. You've had thousands of years of practice. I've only had this brain for about forty-seven years. Oops, sorry. Forty-seven years plus whatever a sleepy little trip across time and the universe might add on."

"Although we have had many of your years to develop our abilities, our brains are limited to the amount of information it will process and retain. We have the ability to manipulate some items such as the portals and the craft you have traveled on. There are a number of others, but in time, those will be revealed to you also."

"Then how is the High Scribe able to show me things and allow me to have physical contact with objects eight hundred years in the past."

"Because of the High Scribe's unique position and the responsibility he has in keeping the memory archives, he is awarded that ability from the Council and through the work of our scientists. It is too considerable an obligation for any ordinary inhabitant of my world to be awarded this ability. Therefore, it is passed down to each succeeding High Scribe who shares the same genes and ability."

"Is it possible then, for him, or, someone else to make someone do something they don't want to do? For example, could he put a thought into the mind of a human to hurt themselves, or someone else?"

"Only if they were very weak minded. However, none of the humans brought to my world are weak minded. They were all selected because of their strong abilities or their potential. Any others were put into stasis. No one on my world would do such a thing to a human. We hold all life in high regard."

"Well, it seems the High Scribe may have different values than you. He believes humans are a disease that should be eliminated before they are allowed to spread and infect your people again."

"I do not believe he was referring to humans as a species, but their inherent tendencies. You see, our world in its early stages had a very similar beginning. There were many wars over greed and hate until it almost destroyed our world. There was a revelation and hard choices were made. One of those choices was to weed out of our society the worst of those traits by allowing and, even encouraging, our scientist to manipulate our genes and to control procreation. That process still exists."

"The High Scribe was telling me a little about this, but it seems he himself has retained some of the traits he calls diseases."

"The High Scribe comes from the time before the Cleansing, the removal of those in our society who were the most affected. However, it took scientists many generations to eradicate all the recessive genes believed to be dangerous. There were some, because of position, status, or circumstance who survived to carry the genes. Although rare, there are incidents of some of these traits resurfacing. The inhabitants who show these tendencies, or are found to have them upon examination, are either reformed, or they are removed."

"Does that include humans?"

"Humans who are found to be dangerous and cannot be rehabilitated are not allowed contact with any inhabitant and are put into stasis."

"Does that include children?" Brian asked, afraid of the answer.

"There are no human children," Jack replied. "Humans are not allowed to procreate."

"What about your own children?" Realizing now that he had not seen any since he arrived on this world.

"We do not have children."

"What?" Brian was completely baffled. "I don't understand."

"As I told you, our scientists control our procreation. Before an inhabitant is made self-aware and inserted into our society, there is much training and examination. That ensures there is no disease, the population is maintained at the proper levels, our resources are not used to the extreme, and every inhabitant has a place predetermined in our society."

"Not only does that sound overly sterilized, but it also sounds boring. So, there is no family structure. There's no get together for Thanksgiving, no one to exchange presents with at Christmas, and I would guess the scientists hold the weddings as well. Speaking of that, I was wondering how to tell the sexes apart. The male from the female of your species."

"There is no separation of gender on our world. We carry

both of what you would call the male and female genes."

"And what about love?"

"We have compassion and empathy; that is why we have brought humans and others to our world, in hope that someday, the varied species will have a chance to start again."

"Yet, there appears to be some who don't share that compassion. At least, towards humans. Your own High Scribe has shown a bias, and, there is a young girl who was murdered just a mere eight hundred years ago by someone I believe was other than human."

"That seems very unlikely. However, I will not question your expertise. I look forward to your findings."

"I sensed something new with you when I said I didn't believe the murderer to be human. There is something more about this than you are telling me."

"I will provide you with the answers after you rest. There is still much you must learn as you do. Your abilities are exceeding even what I had expected and it would be good to guard that knowledge. Sleep now."

William N. Gilmore

CHAPTER 10

Brian opened his eyes. The room was dim; however, he could tell he was alone. There were so many thoughts going through his brain, like so much static, it took a minute to concentrate and finally bring the roar down to a slight hiss.

He wanted the room brighter and suddenly, the lights adjusted themselves to a proper level. He hadn't touched the manual controls set up for him. He didn't even say anything, so he knew they weren't voice controlled.

He tried it again, thinking he wanted the lights a little dimmer. And they dimmed. He thought about the lights and they were going up and down in intensity to the point they were almost strobes. He laughed. What else could he do? He was stuck in the closed room and he thought about the portal. An opening appeared in the wall large enough to walk through. He laughed again. Then he got up and walked through it.

Brian found himself outside. It was the first time he had been outside his room unescorted. Nothing had changed. All the buildings were the same, the flying platforms were going here and there, the giant red sun bathed everything in that strange, soft, rose-colored hue he saw when he first arrived. It was all still there. He thought it might all go away like a bad dream if he saw it for himself. That possibly, he had been made to see these things. And that could still be the case, but now, he wasn't so sure.

He thought about going somewhere, anywhere, and one of the unoccupied flying platforms arrived. He stepped on it, but it didn't go anywhere. He tried to think movement. He tried to think speed and steering, but the craft remained there.

"It does not work that way," came the familiar presence in his mind. "You do not think of it going or how it maneuvers, you think of where you want to go. It will take you."

Brian turned, but Jack wasn't there. He was nowhere to be seen. He didn't know how far the telepathic powers could be used. One thing he knew for sure though was that he was hungry.

Suddenly, the craft began a trek around and over some buildings. It wasn't long before it came to a stop at a rather plain looking structure. Probably the plainest building he had seen since his arrival. He stepped down and the craft took off. Apparently, it was responding to another summons.

Brian went to the building and without really thinking about it, although he knew he must have, a portal opened in front of him. He went inside. There were hallways leading in different directions. He didn't know which way to go, much less, why he was here.

"Take the way on your left," Jack sent the thought to him. "I will join you shortly."

Brian smiled. Always with me. Just like big brother, he thought. A slight twinge hit the back of Brian's brain. He smiled again.

Brian started walking to his left and noticed there were several of Jack's species walking towards him with baskets of the fruit. He thought at first, they were walking towards him to give him a basket. However, as they got closer, they made a wide arc around him. They stared at him as they walked past. Brian had that loud static in his head again, but it faded as they got farther away.

Brian walked a little further and noticed there was a window or an opening of some kind where he could look into a large room. Inside this room was a large—blob.

It shook a little. It was like a giant, whale-sized, misshapen glob of Spam. Also, in the room were a number of humans. They were at one end of this thing with carts of the fruit.

Brian thought at first they were feeding this thing. That it must be alive. He didn't see any eyes. There were no legs or arms. The only thing Brian saw was what must have been a mouth. He watched in fascination as several humans stood by this thing's mouth. The cart had been taken away and another was brought in, but this one was void of the fruit. Maybe feeding time was now over. Just as he was thinking that he saw a piece of fruit coming out of this creature's mouth. One of the humans pulled it and placed it on the cart. Another piece of fruit began to come out and another human did the same as the first.

Brian paled at the realization that perhaps what he was looking at was not the creature's mouth. The so-called fruit did not come from a tree or a bush. It came from some strange alien's—orifice.

Brian felt sick and began to turn to go when he felt a presence. Jack was standing there. Again, his small slit gave a cocky little smile.

"I believe you had thoughts of hunger," Jack said. "So, the platform brought you to one of the locations where sustenance is produced. Did you not want to take some with you? Are you not hungry?"

"I don't know if I'll ever eat again!" Brain exclaimed. "What is that thing?"

"It would not be wise not to eat. Your body will not last very long if you do not. This is one of the inhabitants of another world we saved before its sun went, as your scientists say, nova. They have the abilities to absorb energy particles and then produce the items you refer to as fruit. They have no higher mental functions. As to something you can relate, think of an Earth jellyfish without the tentacles."

"Yeah, right. I don't eat what comes out of a jellyfish's rear end."

"However, your species will eat other living beings,"

Jack countered. "You make slaves, pets, and food from creatures that have intelligence. You hunt them and torture them for fun. You dismember them and remove their heads as trophies. Do you see why we were wary to reveal ourselves to you? Why there had not been other civilizations revealed to you?"

"Yes, we are violent. However, as you have told me, we evolved following different paths. My species may not have been able to survive if they hadn't evolved a little violently. And as it appears, my world no longer has time to change. Have you ever thought that maybe if you had helped, we could have changed? That my world could have continued and maybe we might have been friends and—?"

"We could not allow the contamination that might have occurred," Jack interjected. "If your world had changed and become more like mine, then there may have been a chance. But as you say, there was no time."

Brian and Jack went back outside the building where a transportation craft soon arrived. Having boarded the small craft, it remained in its position. Jack asked Brian where he wanted to go.

"I want to go home," Brian said, solemnly, out loud. The craft did not move.

"I'm sorry, but the craft does not recognize your thoughts of Earth. Do you want to go back to your room?"

"No. Is there a place where your people go to be alone

and to contemplate their lives, their thoughts, even their past or future?"

The craft then started a trek away from the city buildings and structures.

"There are several areas we have that are set aside for such purposes. Some are eons old and are not used as much now. For some reason, your species, at times, longs for such areas."

The craft continued traveling over an undeveloped area just outside the city of Jacks. It flew over strange forest of multi-colored vegetation that was neither trees nor bushes. It was more like looking down on tall, intertwined cabbages.

The vegetable forest spread out over all Brian could see, dotted in places with small ponds of the honey-colored liquid. After what he believed to be a half-an-hour of Earth time, Brian noticed the vegetation began to separate and slowly opened to a rocky plain. It reminded him vaguely of the southwest deserts of Arizona and California.

Soon they came to a huge gorge. It made the Grand Canyon look like a line drawn in the dirt. There were many falls of the honey-colored liquid, thousands of feet high, and a river, miles wide in places. The sight was breathtaking.

The craft slowly settled on a large plateau overlooking one of the falls. Brian stepped off and looking around, noticed for the first time there were large creatures flying over the river and among the falls. They looked like—

"No," Brian gasped, "they can't be."

They were Pegasus. Large, winged horses. Some were black and some white while others were shades of blue, red, or brown. They were the mystical animals of Greek mythology. They were here, wings stretched out, flying around the falls and over the river. Some were along the river's bank grazing while others ran along the edges of the gorge. Brian couldn't take his eyes off them. His mouth, open in disbelief.

"Several of these creatures were taken to Earth many of your years ago. We sometimes integrate non-threatening species onto other worlds to give them a chance to thrive and expand their presence in the universe."

"There are stories," Brian began in almost a whisper, "myths, about these creatures in our past. Some interacting with humans. Some were heroes in their own right. Sadly, they must not have been able to endure earthly tenure. I wish they had."

They were a favorite of Sarangerel's," Jack said. "She called them Hiimori. Wind horses. They have no fear and are trusting creatures. They would come to her and sometimes they would even let her ride them over and around the falls."

"Sarangerel? Who is that?" Brian asked.

"She was a friend. She was the one who died eight hundred years ago. She is the reason I chose you."

Brian was stunned. His knees weakened, and he sat on a rock. One that Sarangerel may have sat on long ago.

"I brought her to my world after finding her hidden and barely alive in a village that was raided and destroyed by a tyrannical warlord. She was special, much like you, in her abilities. However, and not surprisingly, it did take her a long while to adjust to the reality of what was happening to her. Her world was filled with stories and myths based more on superstitions than fact. She had no introduction to the possibility of other worlds or space travel. Slowly, she began to trust me and I became her mentor. Then I became her friend. And then— more."

"How did your people take this? Did the High Scribe know?"

"I was very guarded about my feelings. I believe the High Scribe suspected the bond between us was more than what was acceptable. It is possible she was unable to hide her true feelings against his probes. I suspect the High Scribe enacted his own form of justice and had a hand in her death."

Brian slowly stood again. "He was my first suspect as well, but I didn't have a real motive. Now I do."

PART TWO

CHAPTER 11

"Tell me, Jack, just how far do your abilities reach? Can the High Scribe read my thoughts this far away?"

"No, that is unlikely. Even as receptive as he can be, there are limits but do not attempt to test just how far those limits are. He has a very developed mind and even I do not know what his true limit is. You still need more training on subconscious control. We should go back now."

Brian took a final look at the Hiimori, the wind horses before leaving, still amazed. He wondered what other wonders this world held? What other connections between their worlds would he find?

They boarded the craft once more.

"Tell me more about Sarangerel," Brian said, as they began the voyage back.

"Her name means 'moonlight' in her Earth language." Jack continued. "She was a very young girl when I found her. She lost her parents in a warring tribe's raid on her village. She was alone, hurt, and starving. She would not have lasted much longer, but I heard her very clear, allowing me to find her. It was then I knew her mind was strong. She was worth saving."

"What did she do here? I mean, did she have a job or

duties to perform?"

"Over several years of Earth time, her training elevated to a proficiency that caught the attention of the High Scribe. He wanted her as one of his many minions. He wanted to continue her instruction and growth at his personal direction. The High Scribe gets what he wants. She was instructed in the ways of the archives. Soon, she became his top student. Her abilities outdistanced even the most proficient of his human followers."

"If she was such a good student, elevated in her abilities at his instruction, why then do you think the High Scribe would have been involved with her death?"

"Sarangerel and I continued to see each other. Even with the tutelage of the High Scribe, I wanted to expand her mind even more. Share with her things I thought were important. Things both the High Scribe and the Council would not have approved. I showed her things you still would not imagine. I found myself wanting to be with her as often as I could. I found myself with—emotions."

"And that is something your people are not supposed to have, or at least, show," Brian recalled the conversations with both Jack and the High Scribe. "Did Sarangerel share these emotions?"

"Yes. We shared many intimate moments together."

"You mean you had—relations? I didn't think you did that or that it wouldn't work between our different species?"

"We did not have a physical bond. It was more intense than that. We shared our minds, our innermost thoughts. At times, we were as one. It was an awakening of souls. Giving, taking, sharing, and knowing of the other."

"I think I understand that kind of bond," nodding his head, Brian had a remembrance of his own. "Didn't she have contact with other humans? Didn't she make human friends while she was here?"

"She did not relate to the other humans here and I was the only contact she had other than the High Scribe. She told me she did not trust the High Scribe, that she was able to feel or sense some hidden things deep within the mind of the High Scribe; dark, dangerous things."

"Then I will need all the training and insight you can give me. For both of us. Is there is anything else I can do, anything that might give me an edge?"

"You must keep both your mind and body strong. You must keep yourself nourished."

"Somehow, I knew that was going to come out. Ugh! I don't want to think about it coming out. Well, I guess I've done some worse things in my life. It's funny what you'll do when you are really hungry."

The craft continued with the pair in relative silence until it stopped outside the archives building. They both went to Brian's room. Brian hadn't even noticed the portals were opening without any conscious thought from him. He just thought Jack was doing it.

After entering, Brian noticed there was a large bowl of fruit on a table. He gave a small chuckle and grabbed the bowl offering one to Jack. Jack didn't take any and squatted on his three legs as Brian sat on the couch eating away at the fruit.

"Just for my own dignity, I am going to continue to refer to this—whatever this stuff is, as fruit. And how come I never see you eating any of it?"

"We are of a higher intelligence here on my world. You will not see us eating something that comes from the rear end of another creature."

Brian sat there with his mouth open for a few seconds.

Jack's slit turned up slightly and his eyes actually crinkled a bit.

Brian burst out laughing. It was the first really good laugh he had in a long time. After he was able to settle himself down a little, Brian looked over at Jack and began to laugh again.

"Okay, you got me on that one," Brian began, a few chuckles in-between some of his thoughts. "What is it you do eat?"

"Humans," came Jack's answer.

Brian stopped laughing, his eyes got big.

"Got you on that one, too. It was something hidden in your mind from when you first saw me. A question you were not sure you wanted an answer to. No, we do not eat humans or any other creatures."

"We need to work on your humor," Brian said, shaking his head. "I recalled scenes of an old science fiction horror story. One involving aliens and a cookbook for humans."

"Yes, however, you were also able to block out any other thoughts that may have been in your mind at the time. You are progressing very quickly."

"Thanks. But just to ease my mind, what do you eat?"

We do not eat as you would think of eating. We absorb an energy given off from the very core of our world through the spires you see in the city. We must go through a full rejuvenation of the energy around every six to seven hundred of your years. That is why we must return to our world from wherever it is we might be on a mission or in exploration. We must stay exposed to the spires for a period before the rejuvenation is complete. That time varies depending on how long we have been away or the age of the subject."

"You're like a rechargeable battery. What happens if you can't recharge? What happens if you can't get back?"

"We die. It is a slow and painful death. There have been instances when my people have been unable to rejuvenate because of age or distance. Explorers have been found with their ships disabled in space, not able to return in time. The sights were horrific."

"It sounds a lot like a heroin junkie not able to get his fix for his addiction," Brian recalled, having worked a number of drug cases.

"It is much more than an addiction, it is life."

"Yes, I didn't mean to be insensitive or to lower the importance of your situation to that of Earth's drug addicts. I'm sorry. I am still learning."

"Yes, as we both are."

"So, you are rejuvenating now?"

"For us to rejuvenate, we must be in contact with the spires. I have had minimal contact with the spires since we have arrived. That time will come. But for now, it is time for you to rest and to receive further training."

Brian went over to the bed. "I want to thank you for sharing your story of Sarangerel. I think I understand much more now. I will do my very best to find out what happened and to make sure there will be justice for her."

Brian closed his eyes for the long instructional sleep.

"Justice is for the civilized, my friend," Jack said. "Revenge and punishment are for those who *really* want something done."

CHAPTER 12

Jack spent more time with Brian on this session of his education. This was the most important lesson Jack could give. He had not completed it with Sarangerel before she was killed. He did not realize the deadly consequences of it at the time. He failed her. He had not protected her as he promised. He would not let that be the case with Brian.

During a brief break in Brian's lesson, Jack took one of the flying disks to a very special spot at the large gorge area he had gone with Brian. It was the spot where Sarangerel felt more alive and at home than any other. They would spend a lot of time there. She made it special for him as well. It was the place where he first felt the emotions. He liked them.

He opened the small box he brought with him. It had been a present from her. A very ancient device of his world that she acquired from a scientist. He placed it on the ground. A life-sized hologram appeared. It was Sarangerel. She was smiling. She laughed. She danced. The hologram reached out towards him with both hands.

Jack could still feel her real hands on his face. He could feel the warmth and the care of her touch. A name she called him when he first found her, rang in his mind.

Khünbish. In her language, it meant; not a human being. It was not an insulting name. It was more descriptive. It was a name sometimes given to children of her culture to ward off evil spirits who wanted to steal the soul of the child or to cause mischief. Jack thought how ironic it was because it was Sarangerel who had stolen his soul. Jack continued to watch the hologram loop. A tear, a single, honey-colored tear, came from one of his eyes.

*

Jack returned to Brian's room and continued with the training of his sleeping friend. It was more than training that he would need before his next encounter with the High Scribe.

Soon, Jack knew he would have to go for rejuvenation. The instructional sessions were draining a larger amount of his energy than he had thought. He was in no danger. Yet. However, he could not afford to take the needed time that would be required. The instruction of Brian was too important at this stage.

Even as far as Sarangerel had advanced, her young age proving to be a benefit in her tutorage, Brian was naturally so much more intuitive and yet, guarded. Brian was born into a different world than hers, with years of experience that would need to be overcome.

It was not so much to overcome Brian's experiences, as it was to get around them. He had set up sturdy walls over the years to block certain feelings and things he did not wish to remember. Yet, these things helped to make up Brian's psyche. Things that made Brian who he was. Things that gave him his drive. Even if Brian was unaware of it himself.

After a long while, Brian awoke, refreshed as always and hungry. He was happy Jack was still there. Jack told Brian to nourish himself and to hurry with his hygiene customs. There was much to do and things for Brian to see.

Brian was always excited to see and learn new things about Jack's world. Sometimes his imagination would run wild with things he read about in science fiction books, about strange worlds and even stranger aliens. Nothing matched reality though. He was actually living it.

William N. Gilmore

CHAPTER 13

Jack had Brian meet him outside when he was ready. When Brian came out, he was dazzled. The sky was dark and the city was lighted in so many ways. It was almost like a carnival. It was the first night Brian had seen while he was on this world.

Jack had one of the crafts standing near and they both got on. The craft took off away from the city. Brian's gaze was at the sky. Unfamiliar stars shone with a brightness that put a natural light on the land. Two crescent moons of different sizes hung in the sky as well. One giving a soft, rosy reflection of the sun and the other, smaller moon was almost blood red.

"There will be another moon coming up in a while," Jack said, looking at Brian as he craned his neck up trying to see the whole sky. "It is larger and paler than either of these. There are several cities there as well. You would think of it more as a small planet than a moon. The other two do not support life and are barren, much like your own moon."

"Might I have a chance to visit your sister world?" Brian asked.

"We will see."

They arrived at the gorge in a short while and Brian was amazed. The falls and the river were glowing. Some property within the honey-colored liquid gave it a luminescence that came from within. It wasn't a reflection.

"How does it do that? What makes it glow like that?" Brian questioned, not able to take his eyes away.

"It is part of who we are. It always has been. It gets its energy from within our world. The same as The People do."

"It is so beautiful."

"The old legends of my world say it was made from the tears of The Ancient People at the time of The Cleansing."

"And what would you say?"

"I would say that is many tears. I am happy you enjoy the view, but that is not the only reason we are here. Your training is almost complete. I want you to think about Sarangerel. About her death. I also want you to block those thoughts right now from anyone else getting them. Especially me."

"Alright. I'll see what I can do."

Brian was thinking about the head wound Sarangerel received. How someone may have made the strike that killed her. He could feel a poke in his mind. It wasn't hard to stop it. The poke became a jab and then the jab became more aggressive, but Brian was able to just brush it away.

"That's good. Very good. I am going to try something different. Concentrate on Sarangerel. Think about her death. Think about the person that could do such a thing."

Brian again was focused on Sarangerel's murder.

However, there was something coming at him from another direction. Something was trying to dig at both Sarangerel and something he did at the police department. He was able to block the intrusion into both.

"Again, that was good. You have learned well. Just one more time, please."

Brian was focused. Nothing was getting into his mind unless he wanted it to. He barely had to give any effort to stop it.

"Tell me about the death of your wife," Jack blindsided Brian.

All the walls that Brian put up to stop Jack's test came tumbling down. Not all the way, but enough of it.

"That's not fair," Brian said, shaking his head and turning from Jack.

"You must be able to continue the blocking of your thoughts beyond what emotions you are experiencing. You must not allow anyone to get into your mind because you failed to keep your guard. Even one weakened moment may be enough for someone to gain an advantage. You must exercise your abilities as much as possible."

Brian turned back to Jack. "Yes, you are right. I won't allow that to happen again."

"There is one other thing that I wanted to share with you. I want you to know Sarangerel as well as I did. I want you to understand her so that even in some small way, it may help you."

"It would be my honor to know her, however, I do not believe that anyone could ever know her as well as you have, nor would I want to. That is something that is still shared between you and Sarangerel. No one has a right to get in-between that."

"Thank you, my friend. Then I will surrender my thoughts to you and allow you will go as you please. Put your hands on my head."

Brian took a few steps forward "Did you learn this from a Vulcan?" He placed his hands on the large, alien head of his tutor and friend. Jack, in turn, placed his twenty fingers around Brian's head. As soon as he did, Brian's mind was filled with chaos. As he settled, he found he was in a village on fire. People were running, screaming. He saw through the eyes of the young, frightened Sarangerel. Somehow, he was witnessing her life and he knew what he was seeing.

She was running from barbaric horsemen who were slaughtering her people. She was not running away from her village, trying to save herself, but to the family hut. She ran as fast as she could to get to her parents. People were falling, being cut down, butchered. She was knocked down by one of the horses but was not trampled by the hoofs. She was able to get up and limped to her hut.

Her father was outside the hut, lying on the ground next to four dead raiders. His bloody sword in his hand and bow by his side, his quiver empty. There was an arrow in his neck, another in his chest. She ran into the hut calling for her mother. She was there. Standing with a child in her huge belly and a sword of her own. Upon seeing Sarangerel, her mother dropped the sword. She grabbed Sarangerel and took her to a far section of the hut.

In a corner were some baskets sitting on a plain blanket. She hurriedly knocked the baskets out of the way and grabbed the blanket. There was a flap of twigs and skins. She moved this and uncovered a small, deep hole. Sarangerel's mother pushed her into the hole, instructing her to be very quiet no matter what she heard, not to come out of the hole unless she came to get her. The flap was replaced and Sarangerel's world became dark. She sat in the hole with her arms around her legs, hearing her mother replacing the blanket and baskets. She could hear everything going on in the hut from inside the hole.

After a few minutes, she heard her mother yelling and screaming. She heard the clanging of swords. Then there was silence. She sat in the hole for a very long time in that silence. She was too scared to come out. She hoped her mother would come and get her. She remembered seeing her father. He had fought to protect his home, his family. She remembered her mother's face, seeing it for what may have been the last time, as she covered the hole. As she left to protect her.

She was hurt and scared and hungry, but worse than that, she was alone. Sometimes she slept. Most other times she would just listen. She spent days in that hole. Her hunger and the strain on her muscles were no match for her fear and the insistence of her mother's orders.

She would have remained there, starving except for one day when she heard someone in the hut. She prayed it was her mother. She tried to reach out, calling for her in her mind as she had done over the days in the hole, scared to be heard by anyone else.

Someone was doing something above her. She heard the movement of things inside the hut, then the sounds of things being drug out of the hut. Soon she heard someone removing the baskets, then removing the flap.

Although there was little light in the hut, it was blinding after being in the dark hole for so long. She squinted and tried to focus on the face. At first, she saw her mother. She was thrilled and cried out. She made a great effort to get out of the hole, but her weakened muscles, as well as her injury, would not allow her. A hand reached to help her. It was not her mother's hand. It was not the hand of a raider. It was the hand of something else.

She was lifted out of the hole but could not stand. As she looked up from the floor of the hut, she saw what had helped her. It was something she had never seen before, however, she was not scared. Not of the raiders and not of this creature. She knew that she would be safe. She had been told this in her mother's voice. She did not hear it. It came from somewhere deep in her

94

mind and enriched her heart. It was strong and comforting.

"Thank you, Khünbish," Sarangerel's weak and dry voice struggled to say in her native Mongolian tongue, just before she fainted.

William N. Gilmore

CHAPTER 14

Jack released his hold on Brian and took a few steps back. "That is how I came to find Sarangerel. I heard her calling out for her mother with her mind."

Brian shook his head. His legs were wobbly. The connection with Sarangerel had been so real, he checked himself for the injuries she had sustained. He even felt her hunger. Moreover, he felt the tragic loss of her parents.

"That was intense," Brian finally said. "How long were we connected?"

"Just a few minutes of your Earth's time," came the startling answer.

"But I spent—or rather, Sarangerel spent days in that hole. I felt every second of it. I lived with her fear and pain that whole time, even her thoughts."

"The information was available at an even faster rate, but I was afraid you would not be able to comprehend it all. Your abilities are still exceeding anything I had hoped or believed possible. We will continue this again soon. There is much she can show you."

As they started back, Brian looked out and saw the huge red sun reflecting off the far-away, clear domes of the city, making them shine like star rubies in a ring. A giant moon was coming over the horizon. It was a pale, pinkish color. He laughed. He was looking at a world with alien life from a world with alien life, but he was the one who was the alien.

Brian looked again at the large moon. It gave him a strange thought. Something that suddenly made him question what he had been told about his own world.

"Jack, when we left my world, you put me in that special pod and had me sleep for a very long time, so I would survive the long journey."

"Yes. That is correct."

"But you told me everything on my world died off three hundred years *after* we left. How would you have known that?"

"There are other ships, explorers and scientists who travel faster or through different segments of space than what my ship is capable of being able to do. Information was given to the Council about your world before we arrived. It was relayed to me for the first time in the Council's chambers. I then relayed it to you as I was instructed."

"You were unaware of what had happened to the Earth until we went before the Council?"

"That is also correct."

"And, the High Scribe is a leading member of the High Council?"

"Yes. He is the member of the Council from whom I

received the information about Earth. It was his thoughts I translated for you."

"And we now believe he is the prime suspect in the murder of Sarangerel. How easily do your people lie? How easy is it for one of your people to lie to the rest and to be able to keep it from becoming known?"

"It is not our nature to tell untruths."

"And your people don't commit murders either. Or do they?"

"You do not have facts to support that theory."

"Not yet. Nevertheless, you know, just as well as I, that he was most likely responsible. You've known it for a very long time. He is evil. He is using his position on the Council and as High Scribe for his own agenda. I believe Sarangerel knew it too. That may be one of the reasons she is dead."

"Yes, I believe in some way he is responsible, "Jack admitted. "He is very powerful in his position. The Council usually bows to his will. I am afraid he is changing the very core of our society. There are some who support him and share his beliefs, and then there are others who will not take any stand. However, there is a growing number who believes he is leading our world back to the time of The Cleansing."

"He is hiding much more than the death of Sarangerel," Brian reasoned. "I sense he is being deceptive with me. I am having a hard time believing that all the people of Earth are now gone. In only three hundred years? I know we had problems, but we're better than that. We find ways to overcome adversity, even with our own faults. I don't want it to be true. I don't want to believe him, even if there is the slightest chance for it to be true."

"There are many truths out there we do not want to be true," Jack stated. "However, they are true, and we must live with the truth."

"And a lie cannot be the truth unless you ignore it or allow it. And if he is lying, we don't have to live with the lie, we must expose it. Just as you want me to find and expose Sarangerel's killer."

"Yes. She and The People deserve the truth."

"And if he is lying about that, why can't he be lying about Earth?"

"He could, but we need evidence to expose the lies."

"That is why you have brought me here."

"And it was the right decision."

"And with that in mind, there's something else I've been wondering about. Why would he allow there to be so many humans in stasis, supposedly waiting for the day they can be returned to Earth after it rejuvenates, if there really is no problem with Earth?" What is his agenda?"

Jack did not have any answers.

CHAPTER 15

The craft arrived at the archives a short time later. As Brian and Jack stepped off, many other crafts arrived at the landing platform. One contained the High Scribe.

Brian was attempting to ask Jack what was going on, but there was a lot of noise in his mind. The last thing Brian read clearly from Jack was "My ship—go."

Two of the non-Jacks, took Jack by the arms and placed a device on his head, covering his eyes. Immediately, Brian lost the psychic communication with Jack. They placed him on one of the craft and the three of them left the platform, the destination unknown to Brian.

The High Scribe turned to Brian. "You will surrender yourself for rehabilitation. You and your thoughts are a danger to The People and to yourself."

"You are the real danger to your own people," Brian threw the thought back at the High Scribe. Making sure he was blocking the thoughts he wanted, Brian formed a plan and shot out more thoughts at the High Scribe and the remaining non-Jacks.

The non-Jacks raced to stand before the High Scribe in protection, and the High Scribe himself floated back several feet, but Brian had tricked them. Instead of running at the High Scribe in an attack as he had let them read, he ran to one of the remaining craft and took off from the platform. The High Scribe and the non-Jacks were confused and stunned. That allowed Brian a chance to get away. At least, for the time being.

*

Brian had the transportation craft take him to where the spaceships were docked. He wasn't sure it would work. He was afraid the craft wouldn't understand, or it could be overridden by the High Scribe. It wasn't.

He had caught them off guard and was able to get the head start he needed. They would have no idea where he was going. Once he got to Jack's ship, if he got to Jack's ship, he wasn't sure what he would do. The only thing he knew right then was he must keep his mind blocked. Whatever else he did, that had to be the primary defense to keep from being found. Jack had taught him well.

He got to the ship, or rather, to the ships. There were a large number of ships at the dock. They all looked alike. He had no idea which one belonged to Jack. He didn't know how he was going to locate it. He couldn't ask. All the non-Jacks didn't know Jack as Jack. However, they may know the human, Brian Douglas as being wanted. He would have to be very careful.

Brian got back into his detective mode. He tried to reason how he could find the one ship out of hundreds. After just a few minutes, he figured it out.

Ship's had names, Brian recalled. Usually named after something or someone. Could it be that easy? Then he thought it.

"Take me to the Sarangerel."

Nothing happened.

"Take me to the Khünbish."

The craft failed to move.

Maybe he was wrong. Maybe it didn't have a name. On the other hand, maybe Jack had named his ship something in his own language that he would not know. There were too many possibilities. He put his cop mind into overdrive.

There was something, something in the back of his mind. He looked up at the spaceships. *Pegasus? Wind horses?*

It hit him. "Take me to the Hiimori," Brian called out.

The craft took him right to a platform where a single ship was docked. It was as big as a bus and cigar shaped. A long, sloped gantry went up to a hatch. A real door-like hatch, like the ones on airliners. He stepped off the transportation craft and started up the gantry. There was no one around, however, he wasn't sure if he was being watched. He didn't feel any intrusion or attempts at reading his thoughts, so he continued.

As he approached the hatch, it opened. He wasn't sure if he had done that, if someone was coming out, or if it was automatic. He froze. There was nowhere for him to hide or run. Instinctively, his hand went down to his right side, preparing to draw. He wasn't wearing a gun.

The hatch was fully open. No one came out. Brian moved up to the hatch and took a quick peek in. There was no one in sight. He waited just a minute and didn't hear anything either. He entered the ship, walked a few steps, and the hatch closed behind him on its own.

CHAPTER 16

The ship was large on the inside. It seemed like a lot of wasted space. Brian slowly made his way around, not knowing if there was anyone inside. Not knowing what he would do if there was.

He came to the area in the front of the ship that had a multitude of instruments. There was even a large window. This obviously was the control center. Some instruments looked familiar and some could not even be guessed at for their function. There were several seats. One appeared to be made for a human to fit. The other was for Jack or someone of his species. The other, not so much. He continued to check the ship but found no one on board.

This is where Jack told him to go. If that's what the last communiqué had meant. He didn't know if he was supposed to wait on him, which was unlikely, since he seemed to be under arrest or detention and there was no idea when, or if, he would be released. There did not appear to be anything here that was left by Jack for him. He went back to the control center. He went to the seat made for a human and sat to think out his next course of action.

As he sat, the seat pulled him into it. As much as Brian

struggled, he could not get free. He felt that tingling feeling as he did when he first encountered the portal, only this time, it was many times more powerful. It wasn't painful, just strange.

He didn't feel it, but he could see through the window that the ship was moving. The ship was pulling away from its parking place. The dock was now far below and soon was out of sight. In just a couple of seconds, Brian found himself looking down on the whole planet. He was able to see the moons and far off, a large red sun. Brian was in space. He had been in space before, he just hadn't seen it. He was mesmerized. Pictures didn't do it justice.

Brian jumped as Jack's voice hit him. He looked around but did not see his alien friend. The voice spoke out once more. 'Push the button to your left'. Brian looked to his left and saw a single console with one button on it. He started to reach over to push it when he was startled again by Jack's voice. 'Push the button to your left'. He reached over and pushed it.

As soon as he had pushed it, the seat let Brian go. In front of him, Jack's full-sized image appeared in a hologram much the way Sarangerel's image had appeared from the small box Jack had at the gorge. Jack spoke to him in a voice he could hear. It wasn't something he expected, and it caught him off guard.

"Hello, my friend. I have prepared this and other instructions for you in the event circumstances would not allow me to join you. Certain safety precautions were made so only you would be able to activate the controls. The ship is on a set course, for now, one I previously prepared in case there were problems. There are instructions here on how to operate this ship, there is food for you, and there are other things on board that may be of use. It would be my belief that I am not with you because I am dead or there has been a decision for me to be rehabilitated or maybe, even be put into stasis. This decision may have been made by the Council, but most likely, it came from the High Scribe. And possibly even without the Council's authority or knowledge."

"Jack, can you hear me, or can this thing respond to me?" Brian had to ask, not knowing for sure if the image was interactive.

The visualization continued. "I may not be able to communicate with you any further. There is a device that may be in use to block the telepathic connection and they may have moved me to a location that is also fully blocked. To continue your investigation into Sarangerel's death would be dangerous for you. However, I believe that is the key. Good luck to you my friend. Thank you. To learn how the ship operates and for additional instructions, go to the room behind you and open the portal. Once inside there will be a table with a device on it. Put the device on your head, lie on the table, and tell it to begin. This will only take a couple of your Earth's hours."

The hologram vanished. That was the end of the message

Jack had made for him. Brian did not hesitate. He got out of the seat and went to the room. The portal opened, and he went in. It was the same room he had been in when he first saw Jack.

On the table was the device. It wasn't hooked up to anything. It looked like a large colander with wires and headphones attached.

Brian picked up the device, got on the table, and put it on his head. He was surprised to find that it fit. He felt a little silly. Nothing was happening. He forgot. He had to tell it to—

*

Brian woke with the device still on his head. He took it off, putting it on the table. He exited the room and went to the dimly lighted control station. The lights brightened immediately at his presence. "Lights," Brian said in his mind as he sat, "fifty percent." The lights around the control compartment dimmed. He looked out the window. The ship traveled to just where it had been programmed to go. He was behind the smaller of the moons of Jack's world. He gave a few more commands and the ship took off.

Brian received more than just instructions on how to operate the ship. Jack provided him with information that would help him make decisions on his next move. Jack had not told him to stop his investigation into Sarangerel's death. He just told him it would be very dangerous. Jack left all of the other options up to Brian.

Brian was amazed at the knowledge placed in his mind. And yet, this was just the first session. Jack arranged for there to be four sessions so as not to overload Brian's inferior brain. Each session was set up in an order Jack believed Brian would need for the operation of the ship, equipment, maps, and a network of friendly contacts, among others. The ship had also been set up to be able to receive and operate on Brian's English vocabulary of audible words and thoughts. Jack had been busy.

The contacts were people Jack trusted and were of a like mind when it came to believing the High Scribe was a danger to them all. Something that was more than obvious to Brian now.

Brian had time to eat and receive another session of Jack's instruction before he reached his destination. Before heading into the room, he looked out through the window. "NASA, eat your heart out," he said out loud.

William N. Gilmore

CHAPTER 17

The ship landed on the larger of the moons of Jack's world. Moon was a strange word for a world with an atmosphere, vegetation, and inhabitants; at least, to Brian. The landing location was not at one of the cities nor was it even on any landing platform. It landed in a small ravine several miles from, well, just about everything.

One of the things Brian learned about Jack's ship was that it was equipped with its own small transportation craft. A shuttlecraft, per se, and it was located in the belly of Jack's ship. As he boarded the small craft, a ramp automatically opened to the surface of the strange moon.

Brian thought of the location he received in his instructions and the craft took off. He was nervous, to say the least. Here he was, an outsider; a way outsider. These were Jack's own people. People whom he trusted. And Brian, a human, would be asking them to trust him, and possibly, a whole lot more.

The craft didn't go to a city. It didn't go to some building. It landed on a flat plain among what might be called bushes and shrubs. Different from the vegetation on the planet. Brian was where he was supposed to be, but he had no further instructions from this point. He looked around and saw nothing that would indicate why he was there.

Brian felt a presence. "Hello, is anyone there?" He kept his guard up.

There was no answer. He was just about to step off the craft when he got the message.

"Stay where you are, human. Why are you here?"

"I was directed here," Brian sent out, not seeing anyone around. "I have a friend who is in trouble."

"It seems you may be the one in trouble."

"I may very well be, but my friend is in greater danger. He is being held as a prisoner on the planet by the High Scribe."

"Your mind is strong. You are human, but I cannot read your thoughts. There has never been a human whom I cannot read. Why can I not read your thoughts, human?"

"My friend gave me special training. I believe he has sent me to you for your help."

"He must be very talented. Who is this friend of yours?" The unseen sender asked.

"I call him Jack. I do not know his name known by your people."

"And who are you?"

I am Brian Douglas. I am a police detective from Earth. Jack brought me here to help solve the murder of his friend, Sarangerel."

"And have you done that?"

"My investigation was interrupted. However, my main suspect is the High Scribe. I believe that he is in some way responsible if not the actual person directly involved. He took Jack and tried to take me as well, but I was able to escape."

"Will you open your mind to me so that I can verify that you are telling me the truth?"

"And who are you, may I ask?" Brian continued to look around but knew the source was very close.

"On your world, I might be referred to as the brother of the one you call Jack."

Brian was taken aback. "That's not possible. Not by what Jack has told me about The People and your culture."

"It is true. Although we were not born as humans are, we are from the same—stock, as you would say. It was an experiment of a scientist to see, one, if he could do it, and two, if he could make me—"

"Different? Brian asked.

"Enhanced would be a better word."

"And you are known by what name?"

"You may call me as you wish," he said as he came from around a thick bush. The Jack species that he expected, was not. It was something altogether new.

Brian just stared. This creature was about a half foot taller than Jack. The head was more human, almost pear-shaped, but the eyes were larger and wider apart than any human he had ever seen. He had a small nose and a real mouth that was turned up into a smile. There were two legs and two arms. This was a strange cross between a Jack-style creature and a human.

"I received a signal from the ship to meet here. It had been pre-arraigned by my brother and I if there had been trouble on the planet. I did not expect to see a human."

"And I didn't expect to see you," Brain returned.

"Will you open your mind to me now? Allow me to see the truth?"

Brian had trusted Jack and Jack sent him here. Brian's instincts were telling him there did not appear to be any danger. This was the help he was seeking. It was worth taking a chance.

"Okay, but I have a lot of things that have gone into my mind recently. Please go slow."

The hybrid approached the disk and motioned for Brian to step down. As soon as Brian stepped onto the surface, he felt the heavy tug of gravity this moon possessed.

The hybrid placed his hands, both with six fingers each, on the head of Brian. Brian placed his hands on the hybrid's head as well. He removed the barriers he had in place but kept them right on the edge if he needed them quickly.

The hybrid's smile widened. "He has great trust in you. And he values your friendship very much." He let his hands go free of Brian's head. "Thank you, for being his friend and for helping him."

Brian removed his hands also and knew this hybrid creature was telling the truth.

"That is why I am here. He needs your help as well. We need to get him back and expose the High Scribe for what he truly is."

"That will not be easy. We do not know where (there was a truly unpronounceable and unimaginable series of sounds) might be held and the Council will not accept any action against the High Scribe unless there is irrefutable evidence. And with his influence, even that may not be enough."

"Nonetheless, we must try," Brian pleaded.

"You have been branded a danger to our society and are now wanted much as I am, and my appearance will not get us far. There are only a few of The People who I believe we can trust. Maybe even a human or two."

"Jack, and if you don't mind, can we please refer to him by that name, imprinted information in my mind that includes some contacts."

"Yes, I read that as well. There was some information within your mind meant for me. I know who these people are and where to contact most of them."

"I was unaware Jack left you a message inside me."

"One of the things he left for me was to tell you he has confidence in his friend."

"Then what is our next step? Where do we go?"

"We get some more help and then we find—Jack."

CHAPTER 18

Brian secured the shuttle disk in the belly of the ship and the ramp retracted. Jack's brother looked over the modifications Jack made to the ship.

When Brian got back up to the control center, Jack's brother stated, "He provided well for us here. Even changing the seats out."

"Apparently, he did this while I was sleeping, or rather, learning. He must have had some suspicions and a plan he put into motion. I wish he had told me. I could have helped."

"I do not think he wanted to put you in danger. Besides, you needed your training and it is possible you were not ready to hide such secrets."

"I wouldn't have let anyone in my mind that I didn't want. I can now block my thoughts without Jack's help."

"Now, maybe. But you are still learning. As I have seen, you still have some instruction left for you by Jack. I believe it is time you returned to that instruction and I will take us to our destination."

"What is our destination?"

"To a place I am very familiar with and one you will see when we get there."

"In other words, you don't trust me yet."

"In other words, I will do as you have done. I will go to great lengths to protect my friends."

"Very well," Brian said, feeling a bit of a slight. "I'm sorry we didn't get to the part about what to call you. What do you think of the name Asshole?"

"That is almost funny since you are the only one here who has one. What about a simple name like John or Bob?"

"Why not Sue or Betty?"

"I do not care. It is your choice. Just remember, if you get into trouble, call the name you think I will answer."

"I think John will work nicely," Brian gave in. "I'll see you in a few hours," he said, entering the small room.

"Sleep well," John sent, giving a grin."

*

John sat in the chair that was obviously put there for his form. As he did, the hologram activated.

"Hello, my brother," Jack's hologram said. "I hope your initial contact with young Brian went well. If you have been allowed to unite with his thoughts, you will know he is my friend. Be patient with him. He is human after all. However, I have been able to guide and instruct him and his abilities are far beyond those of other humans, even some of our own people. He still has some sessions that will be beneficial to him and you. It is important to remember that what needs to be done is for all The

118

People as well as for the humans."

"You were always the one looking out for everyone else," John said to the image.

"If the plan I have is to be successful, you must trust what I am doing is right. Neither the Council nor the High Scribe must be allowed to stop this. Open their eyes. Take care of my friend Brian. Help get him home. For safety, I have provided him with only some of the information detailing the new plan. I will also provide you with part of it as well. Together you will be able to complete what needs to be done."

"I plan to get us all home safe, brother. Including you."

A section of the control panel in front of him opened and a device extended out to within just a few inches from him. John placed his face against the contact points and closed his eyes. After a few minutes, John opened his eyes and removed his face from the device. It retracted back into the panel.

"The information I have just provided will help you with your tasks at hand." Jack's ghost image said. "I doubt if I will be able to assist any further from this point. Be well, my brother."

The hologram disappeared, and John set the course for the ship. It didn't head for the planet. It headed towards an out of the way settlement on the moon they were on.

John set the ship down just out of sight of the settlement. He wasn't ready to advertise his presence just yet. Saying it was a 'settlement' was giving it too grandiose of a name. It wasn't a city like on the planet. There were no huge, magnificent buildings, no domes, and there were no beautiful fountains. There weren't any transportation craft going all about. In fact, it looked bleak and abandoned. These were not the glass and shiny, metal structures. These were just a few old, rundown looking buildings. Tightly packed.

John started for the settlement on his own. He didn't bother with the shuttle. He left Brian to continue his instructions, believing he would be back before he awoke.

It didn't take John long to get to the edge of the settlement. It hadn't changed. It was just as he remembered, although he hadn't been back in a very long time. He kept in the shadows and along the edges of the buildings. He made his way to a set of buildings that would give him cover and a good view. He waited.

After a while, John went to the edge of one building and looked around. Again, no one was present. He was about to go back to his hiding place when he felt the presence. It was too late. A gun, or what might loosely be referred to as a gun, was placed to the head of John.

"Welcome home." was the greeting from the gun-toting non-Jack.

John slowly turned. With a smile reminiscent of another, John said, "Thank you."

The non-Jack holding the gun-thing felt an altogether

new presence. It was too late. Brian had a gun, a real, Earth-made, semi-automatic pistol at the head of the non-Jack.

"Would you be so kind as to drop the weapon you have pointed at my friend's head," Brian asked.

The non-Jack did as he was requested.

Brian looked at John and said, "This is what is known as a rescue. We were supposed to be doing this for Jack. Did you get a little sidetracked?"

"I really did not need the rescue but thank you anyway."

"From my position, it looked like just another second or two and your head would have been scattered all over the surface. Or would it have been disintegrated, or maybe, vaporized with that strange weapon?"

"I do not think he would have done that. It would have been a terrible waste of his creative talents. Brian, meet my father."

William N. Gilmore

CHAPTER 19

"Your father?" Brian questioned. "And on whose side is he on? You, trying to sneak up on him and then, I find him with a gun to your head. We have dysfunctional families on Earth and they star in some far-out reality shows, but this, this is about as far out as they go."

"What is he talking about? Where did this human come from and why is he here?" John's father asked. "And would you have him put down that silly looking thing."

"This silly looking thing could have blown your silly looking head right off that silly little body of yours."

John looked at Brian strangely.

"I'm sorry, was I being just a little overdramatic?"

"No," said John. "It's that you are communicating in our language."

"Your language? I do not know your language."

"Apparently, Jack had that in the instructions you just received. And where did you get that?" John asked, pointing at the Smith and Wesson 9mm pistol Brian still had in his hand.

"A storage area was revealed to me. There were several Earth weapons present that I have an expertise in. I did not receive any training in the use nor can I use my five-fingered hands on your weapons."

"So, would you mind putting it away?" John asked.

"Is it safe?"

"Yes. We need to go inside. There will be much to talk about."

Brian put the weapon in a belted holster that had been supplied along with his human garments. Jack had even included his precious fedora as well.

"Before we go anywhere," John's father stated, "would you please tell me what is going on. I still want to know who this human is. I am not about to—"

"Yes, you are. We need to go inside, now. That is for everyone's safety," John said matter-of-factly."

The conversation was over. John's father started toward one of the buildings and towards a real door. He opened it revealing a separate building inside. A portal opened, and John and Brian followed him in.

Brian had to do a double take. As plain as the outside building looked, the inside of the concealed building was just the opposite. It was big, clean and it appeared to have many functions. Brian saw what was obviously a laboratory on one side and what might have passed as a mechanical shop on the other. There were many other things he did not understand. There were humans and non-Jacks working side by side on projects. Just the type of place a mad scientist would drool over.

"Do you have your shield activated?" John asked his father.

"Always," came the reply. "We are safe."

"The High Scribe has taken (again there was that unpronounceable sound that was Jack's name, but Brian was able to comprehend it this time, although he still could not pronounce it. Even so, he would always call them by the Earth names he had given them)."

"What do you think he will do with him?" John's father asked.

"I do not think he will rush into anything. There are too many on the Council who are aware of his—shortcomings, and I do not think he would want the Council looking too deeply into his activities."

"I'll ask again. Who is this human who I cannot read? What does he have to do with this?"

"He is a detective who was brought here to investigate the murder of Sarangerel. The Council authorized it, even with the objections of the High Scribe, and (the unpronounceable sound that is Jack) chose him and brought him from Earth. He believes the High Scribe is involved with Sarangerel's death. He has received training to block his thoughts. He is—a friend."

"He has been trained well in hiding his thoughts. However, I am not a detective nor am I from Earth and I already know the High Scribe was involved."

"That may be true, however, the High Scribe and the Council know where your loyalties lie. The Council knows of your—disagreements with the High Scribe."

"What makes him qualified to investigate the High Scribe and why would the Council ever believe anything he would say about one of their own?"

"He was a police detective on his world," John said. "He does not have any loyalties except to the truth. Now, that truth is being manipulated. The investigation has been compromised by the High Scribe who is now the prime suspect. The Council is unaware of his findings so far."

"If you would recall, I was a member of the Council and they did not believe me then about that (unpronounceable screeches that would not be a nice name)," John's father countered. "That led to my exile here on this moon."

"That is true, but the High Scribe has many allies and followers on the Council and you had no proof. Brian is working hard on getting that proof. First, we need to find and release— Jack. And for the human's benefit, would you please call him that. I am known as John and I am sure he will come up with a name for you as well."

"I have a name. Apparently, he can understand and think our language now so, he can use my name."

"He is still human though."

"I have many humans who work with me and they all

know my name."

"And how many times have you yelled at them for not getting it right. Even with the training in our language, they cannot make the sounds that constitute many of our words. They cannot think like that."

"Their brains are inferior. That is why it is essential to have our people work with them. Is there a plan to get your brother away from the clutches of the High Scribe or are you here for some other reason?"

"There is a new plan Jack himself has formulated," John said smiling. "However, you are not going to like it."

"I don't care which plan he uses. If it works and it rids our universe of this High Scribe, I will love it."

"What happened to those emotions your people were supposed to have in check and were prohibited?" Brian asked, dumbfounded. "In addition, what about not having any crime? And why were you exiled to this moon?"

"Shut up, human," John's father said, shaking his head. "I told you," he said, turning to John, "inferior brains."

William N. Gilmore

CHAPTER 20

Brian was sent back to retrieve Jack's ship. As soon as he stepped out of the outer building he lost all thoughts from John, his father, everyone. It was as if the building were empty and he was alone. It must be the shield John talked about. He had forgotten how much he enjoyed the silence.

He had many questions for John and his father. There still had not been any detailed information about a plan. Not from John and not from any of the instructions left by Jack. Wasn't he part of the plan now? He hated being left out of the loop.

Brian parked the ship at a dock just behind the building. As soon as he shut down the ship, a group of non-Jacks and humans came out of the building and put a covering over it. He went back into the building looking for John, homing in on him around the laboratory.

"Jack's instructions did not give a lot of information about a plan," Brian said. "It seems there has been a plan for a very long time."

"There has been a plan in one form or another ever since my father was voted off the Council and exiled to this moon. Long before I became self-aware. Father had his plan, Jack had his plan, father and Jack had a plan, and then Jack found out about me and would not have anything to do with father. Or me."

"What do you mean he found out about you?"

"There are many things you do not know. Some things Jack could not tell you. There are things he still does not know. Father was a very highly regarded scientist. He was also very high on the Council. He and the High Scribe were very close. It was believed the High Scribe was grooming him to become the next High Scribe. However, there was a human female with whom father had a fascination. It caused a divide between him and the High Scribe.

"Like father, like son," Brian said.

"Many cycles ago, father secretly used his own genes and was able to create Jack. He instilled in him what would be unauthorized traits and abilities. The High Scribe became aware of this and kept the information to himself. In doing so, he could not use this information against father without incriminating himself. However, father did not stop there. Later, with the assistance and support of the human female, I was the next experiment. Jack was not supposed to know. Father did not get permission from the Council to conduct the experiments with humans. The High Scribe learned of father's feelings towards the human female, and ultimately, me. Under the demands and pressure from the High Scribe, even with his friends and prestige in the Council, father was removed and exiled. However, not before he was able to move all his work here. This was my home, the place of my self-awareness."

"And the human female, your mother?"

"She lived a very long time for a human. She stayed by father's side her whole life. She became ill from the natural progression of your species and close to death when father was forced to put her into stasis. He could not part with her. He believes someday there may be a way to cure the illness and revive her and return her to him. He used both of their genes in my creation. Jack believes she died. Father never told him the truth."

"Then why are you telling me. You should tell this to Jack, or at least tell him in one of those holograms if you don't want to face him."

"If something should happen to father or me, as his friend, I want you to know the story, so you will be able to tell him in person if the time comes."

"If something happens to the two of you, it will most likely happen to me as well. I am wanted, remember?"

"As am I," John said. "I am not well known, but the High Scribe and several members of the Council want me destroyed as an abomination and a threat to The People. That is why I left this city, my father, and live a life of solitude. However, Jack always knew how to find me or contact me. That is how I knew to meet you where I did. There is a real chance now to end this reign of the High Scribe. Plans were made many of your years ago. It is now time to put them on their path."

Brian and John went into the laboratory area to find John's father. They passed by an area with a large door and Brian asked what that part of the laboratory contained.

"That is part of father's other works. No one besides father is allowed to go in. He doesn't talk about what is in there or what he is working on. Not even to me."

They continued their search for John's father and found him in a work area with another non-Jack and a human working on what looked like one of the guns John's father had held.

They approached while John's father gave instructions to the workers. John's father held up the gun and was inspecting it. It was a beautiful piece. The weapon's characteristics included a long, closed, rectangular barrel with cutouts along the sides where small spheres of multi-colored, glowing lights were encapsulated in its design. It had multiple triggers for several of the non-Jack fingers. There was no cylinder or magazine, but it had a control device with settings. It looked more like several battery-operated squirt guns had been melted along with Christmas tree lights infused within them.

"What exactly do those things do?" Brian asked.

"It depends on what setting you put them on. It could range anywhere from a stun to disintegration," John said. "Father is very skilled at weapon making. They are even considered works of art. He even made one for Sarangerel. One that can be held and operated with the human hand."

"And why would she need one of those?"

"As I said, they are works of art. She commented on their beauty and was fascinated by their abilities. Father made it as a gift to her. Her's was especially beautiful. Humans are not usually allowed to have possession of them. Father, however, believed she may need it someday."

"Do you know where it is now? Brian asked.

"No. It was not among her things after her death and Jack did not take possession of it."

"Your father knew Sarangerel. Did you?"

"No. She died many Earth years before I was self-aware. However, I have seen her in the hologram and the thoughts my brother has shared with me. She was beautiful for a human female. I am sure it reminded father of the times he had with the female human he brought from Earth; my mother. Her name was Eve."

William N. Gilmore

CHAPTER 21

John's father waved them over to the work area. "I am attempting a new modification on one of my weapons. If I am successful, it will be able to not only stun them but have them adhere to my commands."

"You mean like mind control?" Brian asked.

"To some degree. Whoever is stunned will have their thoughts disrupted which will allow the user to give commands that will be followed as if they were the stunned subject's own thoughts."

"That would be a neat trick," Brian said. "How soon before you have that perfected?"

"Well, let me see," John's father said, pointing the gun now at Brian. He pulled on several of the triggers at once.

Brian started to step back. He heard a crackle like cellophane being rustled in a hand and felt a shock like the time as a young boy, he stuck a bobby pin into a wall socket, electrical current running up and down his body.

Unlike the time as a child when he was thrown across the room, this time he was frozen motionless and had a terrible urge to suck his thumb. Nothing else mattered. Nothing else was going on around him. He was alone with his thumb. He put his right thumb in his mouth and made loud sucking sounds. He was happy, content.

The crackling sound returned as he was stunned again, and he had a fog in his mind that took a few minutes to clear. He felt no pain other than a little tingling and his right thumb hurt where he bit it when stunned the second time. He knew he had his right thumb in his mouth, but he no idea why.

"You shot me, you son of a—a—test tube. I know you did, but other than that, I don't remember much. Why did I have my right thumb in my mouth?"

"That is the thought I put into your mind," John's father said. "I wanted to see if it was working yet and give you a demonstration."

"What if it had given me a seizure?" Brian protested. "What if that thing had fried my brain?"

"It was not likely. I had it on a low setting. One your inferior human brain could tolerate."

"Okay, I get it. We all get it. We humans have inferior brains. You do not have to keep reminding me. However, that does not give you permission to shoot me with your experimental weapons."

"I am sorry," John's father said. "I thought that was what I was reading from you. That you wanted to be part of the experiment."

"Not like that, but here is a thought you might be able to

read correctly."

"Although that is physically impossible for us to do, that is not a very nice image," John's father said.

"Neither is being shot and made to look like a fool," said Brian. "Would that thing work on your people?"

"Yes, it would. At a higher setting, of course."

"What I was wondering was if you could make me one of those like you made Sarangerel. Exactly like the one you made for her. Plus, your little addition there."

"Yes, I can do that. The one I made for her was the only one I ever made for a human. It was strange because of your five-digit hand. I still have the plans for it. I can have it ready very soon."

"Good. Thank you. And with your permission, I have a name I can pronounce that I would like to use in addressing you."

"And what is the name human?"

"I believe it would be appropriate if I named you after one of Earth's great scientific figures. A Doctor Frankenstein. I will call you Frank," Brian said.

"That will do then. I will allow you this for being a friend to—Jack and John."

Brian had to really concentrate and not give any hint of the true nature of the name. He was sure he would have been shot again, maybe at even a higher setting, if Frank learned the true nature of Doctor Frankenstein and his creations. He decided to change the conversation. "Now we need to get back to how we are going to rescue Jack from the High Scribe," he said.

"There is already a plan for doing so," John sent. "It is one of many Jack put into motion a long time ago. Long before you were even born. Just in case of times like these."

"Well, I am part of it now," Brian insisted. "I am sure Jack did not even have a clue a human would become such a major part of this so-called plan."

"Do not be so sure," John said, turning his hybrid human-alien mouth into a strange smile.

CHAPTER 22

Jack was restrained on a slab in a room. He could now
see but still wore the device on his head restricting his ability to
receive or send any thoughts. The silence was almost maddening.
It was the first time he could not sense something in his mind
since he became self-aware.

The High Scribe, circling the slab, manipulated a device
he held, and the slab tilted until Jack was in an upright position.
Again, the High Scribe touched the controls and Jack began to
just feel his presence like a flicker of light far off in the darkest
night. It began to grow. Even though it was the High Scribe, Jack
welcomed the contact.

"Your human is more resourceful than I imagined. You
have taught him well. Where is he?"

"He is human," Jack strained to send. "However, he is
not my human. He has his own thoughts."

"He is dangerous," proclaimed the High Scribe. "To all
of us. To our world."

"He is dangerous to your world," returned Jack. "The
world you have made. You have used your position to advance
your own power and agenda. You do not deserve the
title of High Scribe. You are not one of us."

"And they are? Have you not seen what they do to us? How they contaminate us? I tried to warn (the name that was Jack's father) about the human females he brought back from Earth. How he kept them as pets and used them to experiment. Mixing our species. And you, following in his path, continuing the contamination.

"He only brought back one Earth female and she was neither a pet nor an experiment. She was his companion, just as Sarangerel was a companion to me. Humans, though inferior with their abilities and emotions, are not mindless animals. They are still evolving, much as we did. They can be taught."

"But should they?" The High Scribe asked. "And you consider yourself one of us? You have not been told everything. There are many things that have been kept from you. Even your own existence is a violation of our codes. I should have stopped him before you were allowed to become self-aware."

"You will say anything to further your own corrupted agenda. You have allowed hatred and ego to surface in your heart and mind. You are the one who is in violation of our codes. You are a traitor to The People."

"I am not the spawn of an inferior species. I am not the abomination. You chose to support and contribute to that line of progression. I will ask you one last time to tell me where the human is, so we can limit the contamination he might bring upon The People."

"I will tell you something I learned from my friend Brian Douglas, and although it is a physical impossibility for our species, for you, I think it is very appropriate and—

The High Scribe ran his hand over the control and Jack's sending side of the telepathic connection was severed.

"For the good of The People," the High Scribe allowing Jack to read his final comment, said, "I am placing you in stasis. There will be no rehabilitation, no retraining, and no further contacts with any of The People or the humans—ever."

In one of the few rare times Jack ever made an audible response, in the ancient spoken language of The People, he told the High Scribe, "Go screw yourself", and smiled.

William N. Gilmore

CHAPTER 23

Brian held in his open hands the strange and beautiful gun Frank made for him. It was indeed a work of art. It was colder and lighter than he would have imagined.

"This is exactly like the one I made for Sarangerel," Frank said, "with the exception of the added feature you requested. There are things you must remember. The power of this weapon derives from a combination of the chemical reactions with certain matter within a small chamber. There are controls that limit the amount of reaction, however, at full levels, the gun can be unstable and may even destruct. If this happens while you are holding it, the result will not be pretty."

"Are you saying this is radioactive?" Brian questioned, his hands now not so steady, ready to hand off the deadly piece of art. "This thing could have an internal nuclear meltdown?"

"It is not harmful to you as it is and using it will have no side effects. Not unless you point it at yourself," Frank added.

"That's good. When can I test it out? See what it does?"

"We can do so right after I give you some basic instructions. You will notice it has several triggers. The primary ones are for the use of the weapon itself, the others are for the disruption of the thought and control process. It would be best not to confuse them."

"Yeah, I guess there would be no need for thought control if you've disintegrated someone's head."

"Exactly. Now pay attention. There are two controls for the power settings. The left side is for the weapon and the right is for the thought disruption. Again, do not confuse these."

"Check. Left for head disintegrations, right for thumb sucking."

Brian felt the beginning of a tingle in the base of his skull but blocked the full force of the impact quickly before it became close to painful. "Sorry, I'll focus."

"Remarkable. Your abilities appear to be getting stronger every sub-cycle."

"I don't feel any different, although I don't hear the constant buzz like I used to."

"You are able to block out the background now without thinking about it. Part of your subconscious is overshadowing your conscious thoughts, giving you what you need before you even realize it. Just like breathing and muscle control."

"And I still have another session to go. I can't imagine how much more I might need to learn, but it could be anything. Funny though, I don't have any real feeling of urgency in getting it done like the others. It's almost like it's waiting for the right moment."

"That may be part of the new plan," Frank explained. "Of

course, we all had our own ideas of a plan. Mine was just to kill the High Scribe, but I was overruled saying that might cause even more problems. Now it looks like that would have been the easiest cure and we would have fewer problems."

"That's just a little out of your people's nature, isn't it? Violence? Even murder?"

"Did you forget the reason you are here?"

"I am beginning to believe I was brought here for a number of reasons, besides finding Sarangerel's murderer."

"That may be true, although it has not been revealed to me. One day I may be judged as a co-conspirator, but for now, I am just an accomplice in the hiding of wanted fugitives."

"For a world without crime, it seems you are making up for lost time."

"I am afraid we are just getting started, so you may want to get acquainted with your new—toy."

"You are right. No jokes here. I'm ready to give it a try."

"We will go outside for you to test it. It will be much safer there. I will have one of the human assistants bring out a target for you."

"Can't I just shoot at a rock or a board or something?"

"Maybe I did not explain fully. The weapon only works on organic matter."

"That's pretty nasty. Why would you invent such a weapon that will only work on living subjects?"

"Because you want them to be dead or mindless subjects," was Frank's matter-of-fact answer.

*

Frank and Brian, along with one of Frank's assistants boarded one of the flying platforms and traveled about a quarter mile from the lab. John stayed behind to check Jack's ship to see if there was more on the plan and to begin their preparations.

The assistant held a large container in both hands with a cloth draped over it. Frank directed him to place the contents on a flat rock on the ground about twenty feet away. He uncovered a glass beaker and poured the mass onto the rock then hurried back to Frank and Brian. The mass looked like a large, raw ham, sitting on a plate.

"Is that thing alive? Brian asked.

"Not in the sense that you would think," replied Frank. "It is not a creature or an organism. It is an organic creation that has been kept viable for testing."

"Thank goodness. Okay. What do you want me to do now?"

"Do you remember your instructions?"

"Yes."

"Good." Frank opened a case and removed the weapon and held it out to Brian. "Shoot that large rock over there."

Brian looked over at a big boulder thirty feet from them. "But you said it didn't work on non-living items."

146

"Shoot the rock."

Brian shook his head, adjusted the settings on the gun and pointed it at the bolder. He pulled on the primary trigger. Nothing happened.

"Did you disengage the safety? Frank asked.

"What safety?"

"Exactly. The gun will not fire unless it is fired at a proper target. Now, shoot the organic matter."

Brian again held the gun up, aimed at the ham thing and pulled the primary triggers. What happened next scared and fascinated Brian beyond expectation. The gun gave no recoil, there were no beams of light. Only the crackling sound just before it fired.

The mass that had been the ham thing was there one second and gone the next. No explosion, no smoke, no sizzle. It was like a magician's disappearing trick, but without the cape and wand, or the pretty assistant.

When Brian could focus, bewilderment in his thoughts, he asked, "Okay, where did it go?"

"Out of existence as we know it. As if it were never there at all."

"It just vanished. How is that possible?"

"Everything is made of something. It takes that something, in this case, the organic make-up, and reverts it to the pure energy that is all around us. If you want to know where it is, look around you."

"That is too much power for one person to have," Brian said, realizing the potential for abuse."

"Is it any different from you using your Earth gun to take a life? Is not the human just as dead?"

"Yes, but—" Brian was having a hard time wrapping his head around the concept of the power of the gun.

"It is much cleaner. Now, are you ready to try the other settings?"

"You mean the thought control? Who are we going to test it on?"

"That is why I have one of my assistants joining us. He knows why he is here. He has done this before."

"I don't think I want to point this thing at anything living ever again."

"If you follow the instruction I gave you, there will not be a problem."

"Oh, the problem is not in the instruction, the problem is in the execution. And I certainly don't mean that as a joke."

"You are the one who requested I make this for you and I had no reservations about doing so. Moreover, there may come a time you may need it. (The beginning of Jack's name), excuse me. Jack will be depending on you to help him. Besides the High Scribe, there may be others who try to stop you."

"I am not looking to start a war with your people," Brian

pleaded.

"I am looking to prevent a war among The People," Frank replied. "And so is Jack; with your help."

"Very well. Let's get this over with."

"For humans, you can set the controls at about a third of the way. If it were one of The People, the setting would be two-thirds to all the way over."

The assistant stood about ten feet in front of Brian, looking him in the eyes with no expression at all.

Brian looked down at the gun, checking the controls for about the third or fourth time. "Would you mind having him turn around. I don't want to do this with him looking at me."

The assistant turned around and Brian raised a shaking hand and aimed the gun. It took several seconds and a lifetime for Brian to steady and fire the gun. This time, the crackle was followed by a streak, like lightning, emitted from the weapon totally surprising Brian, almost causing him to drop the gun. The beam struck the assistant who seemed to jerk for a second and then became perfectly still.

"You only have about ten of your seconds to give a mental command to the subject," Frank reported.

Brian looked back at the assistant and sent him the thought to turn around. The assistant turned. Brian then sent to him orders to hop on one leg and the assistant lifted one leg and began jumping up and down.

"To immediately stop the thought control," Frank advised, "shoot him again at about half of what you did the first time. Otherwise, the effect lasts about three of your Earth hours."

Brian shot the poor man again knowing how he must feel. At least he didn't tell him to suck his thumb or any other embarrassing thing.

The man stopped jumping, shook his head and walked slowly over to the transport platform without any word.

"There's no lasting effects or damage to the subject then?"

"Not unless you shoot them multiple times in a row, which should not be necessary."

"I should hope not. What about memory?"

"During the effect, there is no memory of what is transpiring. You can plant false memories for that short period, however, there is a loss of time if the effect is allowed to continue for the duration."

"But will they will recall being shot?"

"Possibly. They may not know who was involved or what happened to them if you use stealth. And one other thing of which to be aware."

"Yes."

"The gun contains limited resources. Once it has been drained of its power, it will not work. I do not know for certain how long it will last."

CHAPTER 24

John checked the logs and systems for any other messages Jack may have left. There were no other recordings except the last lesson Jack had prepared for Brian. Only Brian could unlock that information. Maybe it contained more details of Jack's plan. Apparently, anything more would have to come through Brain.

John returned to the lab just as Frank and Brian arrived from their shooting adventure. He noticed Brian stayed a distance away from his father's human assistant and would not look at him.

When John's father and the assistant walked on, he approached Brian. "You shot him with the thought disruptor, didn't you?" John said, more of a statement than a question.

"Yeah, how did you know?"

"Because I felt the same way after I trained with the gun father made for me."

"Does everyone around here get their own ray gun? If those things got into the wrong hands, they could really create havoc in a short time. They are dangerous."

"Father is not only one of The People's most brilliant scientific leaders, but he is also the only one designated, or rather, was designated as Gun Maker from our world. That is why the craft is so special. The knowledge is only allowed within a very select few."

"Does that include the High Scribe?"

"Of course, but the actual expertise for constructing the weapons is permitted to only one person. That is the Gun Maker. It is within itself, a very high station on the Council. Father, as both the Science Advisor and the Gun Maker, held that station within the Council. Only the Guardian of The People is stationed above the High Scribe and my father."

"But since his exile, there must be someone else who has taken his place as Gun Maker."

"There were two. Both died in accidents while trying to construct weapons. It is a very dangerous task and should not be taken lightly. Besides, the training they received had been inadequate."

"You mean your father had not trained them well enough to succeed him?"

"It was not father. He had not chosen an apprentice yet. It was the High Scribe. The databases do not hold all the gun making information. The Gun Maker is the only one who holds the key to make the guns operate.

Father had been an apprentice of the inventor of the process, but the old Gun Maker held reservations about allowing the secret of the process to be used without his permission and guidance. The Gun Maker, after many years of training and study of my father, gave him that knowledge. He has not passed it on yet."

"You have a lot of knowledge of the old days of your father."

"He has told me many tales of his youth, his travels, the struggles of The People, and how things used to be."

"Ah, the good old days. I bet he—" Brian's body suddenly went slack, and his eyes had a blank stare.

"Brian? Are you alright?" John asked. "Brian?"

Brian slowly came back to life like an old phonograph that had run down and was being cranked up again.

"I need—to go—to the ship."

*

Brian went into Jack's ship alone and prepared for the last lesson. He went into the side room and put the strange device on his head as before and lay down on the table. He did not know how long this session would be but made sure he had eaten something and taken care of his personal hygiene requirements.

"Begin," he said to himself, and shut his eyes, however, he did not fall asleep as he did in the previous sessions. "Start," he thought to himself once again. Nothing seemed to have changed.

Brian opened his eyes. He found he was no longer in the room on the ship. He believed he was in the room where the body of Sarangerel had been on the floor although it looked different. She was not there. Neither was the High Scribe, nor anyone else for that matter. He was all alone in the room for the first time. But at what time?

Brian was confused. Was he really in the room or was it a mind projection as before and he was still on the ship? There were a lot of unanswered questions in Brian's mind, however, he knew he was there for a reason. That reason became clear as the portal opened and Sarangerel entered the room. She was alone, and the portal closed behind her.

She made no indication she saw Brian or was even aware of his presence. She walked right towards Brian and he even backed a step, but then, as she continued, she walked right through him.

Brian didn't feel anything. There was no sensation of touching or a meeting of minds. Nothing. He turned and watched her as she went to one of the tables in the room and placed a bag down that had been strapped over her shoulder. She picked up a fruit from a bowl on the table along with a cloth and took a bite.

Brian spoke to her, knowing with some certainty that she would not respond. He was just an observer. There, but not. Like being on the outside, looking in through a window or watching a movie.

The portal opened again, and a non-Jack walked into the room. It was the High Scribe; however, he was not on his small flying disk.

The High Scribe was obviously angry. Brian could not only understand the conversation that went on between the High Scribe and Sarangerel. He felt it.

"If you pursue a relationship with (Jack's native name), then you will find yourself in rehabilitation at best and maybe even in stasis."

"I don't have to pursue a relationship," Sarangerel fired back. "We already have one. It might be something you don't understand. It may be beyond your customs and laws, but it is real."

"He knows this is forbidden. He knows there is no future for the two of you. You are human. You are inferior," the High Scribe said, emphasizing 'inferior'.

"He is my teacher and my guide. I will be his pupil and his companion. And if there can be more, we will find a way."

"No! That cannot be allowed. I will see that he is sent away. That you are placed in stasis where you will not infect anyone else with your human disease. That no human will ever be allowed to infect any of The People ever again."

"It is not an infection. It's—

The High Scribe attempted to wedge his way into Sarangerel's mind. She was almost too late to stop him. He started towards her and she threw the fruit she still held as she jumped to her bag, falling to the floor as she grabbed it.

Brian could only stand there and watch wide-eyed as the intense situation unfolded.

The table between them acted as a barrier. It gave her the split second to retrieve the strange and beautiful gun made especially for her. The High Scribe grabbed the table and was throwing it at Sarangerel just as she blindly fired, turning her head and body from the impact of the furniture. The gun worked just as it was expertly designed. The table was not affected by the strange weapons power, however, where Sarangerel discharged the weapon, partially below the flying table, where the High Scribe was standing, his legs disappeared. His body, protected by the non-organic table, fell to the floor.

Sarangerel lay on the floor. Blood pooled from where the table hit her at the base of the back of her head. Her sightless eyes stared at where the High Scribe writhed on the floor. He did not bleed, the wounds where his legs had once been now sealed. There was no burning, or smoke, or smell. There was no screaming or moans of pain. The High Scribe simply had no legs. It was as if he never had them, yet, he was in shock at the sudden loss.

He lifted himself up on his two remaining arms, looked over at Sarangerel and felt the absence of her presence. She was dead. He had killed her. And Brian could sense he was glad.

CHAPTER 25

Brian was stunned. He just witnessed the murder of Sarangerel. It was as he and Jack suspected. The High Scribe was the one responsible. And in his evil deed, he lost his legs and would now forever be confined to his little flying disk. Little solace for Jack; even less for Sarangerel.

But the horrific scene was not over. The High Scribe reached out with his mind and made contact with two of his human minions. They soon arrived bringing with them a small flying disk that would become the constant companion of the High Scribe. Under instructions of the High Scribe, they removed the table that turned out to be the murder weapon.

While they moved the table outside the room to a large flying disk, The High Scribe floated over to the body of Sarangerel and took possession of the strange instrument of his new disability. He knew immediately from where it came, whose hands crafted it. He also knew he would not stop until he exacted his revenge. He grabbed Sarangerel's bag, placing the gun into it and hid it under his garments that now covered the stumps of his missing limbs.

Brian was soon alone again in the room. Alone that is, with Sarangerel's lifeless body. He alone had witnessed this ancient incident. Somehow, apparently, Jack had never been able to see it, or he would not have needed his help and he would not have brought him to this strange world.

Brian closed his eyes again and upon opening them, found he was once again in the room on the ship. He removed the device from his head and went out into the control room. He immediately saw the ship was no longer on the alien moon but was now in space. There was no one else on the ship. He went to the control seat made for him and sat, but nothing happened. The ship appeared to be pre-programmed for a destination and a purpose not disclosed to Brian. There was nothing further for him to do, so he just watched, and waited, and slept.

*

Brian was rudely awakened to find two humans on either side of him, lifting him by his arms out of the seat on the ship.

He could see the ship was still in space, however, he did not know where in space.

"What is going on here?" he asked. "Who are you guys?"

Neither answered, nor did they give any indication they heard him, and if they did, they didn't seem to care.

Brian was taken to the hatch of the ship and was afraid they were going to toss him out into space. He attempted to break loose of the large men but to no avail.

Brian braced himself knowing once the hatch opened, they would all be sucked out. He slammed his eyes shut and took a big breath, holding it in his lungs aware that the effort would be wasted once he was exposed to the cold and airless vacuum of space.

The hatch opened, but not to space. Brian opened one eye and then the other, releasing the burning breath he held in his lungs too long and just as quickly, taking one in. There was another ship docked with the Hiimori.

The two humans took him into the other ship and released their hold on him, continuing to stand by his side.

Welcome to my ship and to my home," came the voice in his head as he saw an ancient looking non-Jack, one even older than the High Scribe, rise from the command chair in the control room. "I am, or rather, I was at one time, known as the Gun Maker."

"The Gun Maker?" Brian busted out in his own audible voice so loud, the other humans jumped. "I thought you were dead."

"That bit of information may have been circulating along with many other rumors for some time, and I am not about to dispute them when it assists me in keeping a low profile and out of some of my enemy's minds, however, here I am."

"Yes, here you are, and so am I," said Brian defiantly. "Why have I been forcibly removed from my ship?"

"First of all, it is not your ship. The owner is a friend of mine and for whatever he sees in you human, he has requested

I assist you with certain—shall we say, tasks. And second, you have not been harmed. You are not a prisoner as my friend undoubtedly is. It is important I take certain precautions and not expose—"

Brian could feel the attempted probing of certain areas of his mind by the Gun Maker and had already used the training and the techniques taught to him by Jack to block any intrusion.

"You are very unique in your abilities human. I have met only one other who could come close to your level of mental function. She was a very special human too. In many ways."

"You mean, Sarangerel," Brian stated.

"Yes."

"Then you have been in some kind of contact with Jack since I have arrived. Were you not aware of his abduction by the High Scribe?"

"Yes. Moreover, I have received updated information from other loyal sources about what has transpired. There was a prearranged signal that precluded a series of circumstances that led to this meeting. These have been in place for many of your Earth years. Recent events have brought the situation to a head. It just so happens you were the human chosen at this time to be a part of this—adventure."

You mean rebellion?"

"You may call it whatever you wish, however, it is time to make changes within our social structure so that we can first, survive, and second, grow as a society. It is not in our nature to question authority. Moreover, there are forces at work that would rather see my world inhabited by a sterile and docile population, ruled by those with the power to enslave us and do our thinking and decision making for us."

"We have those on my world as well. Most are called dictators, sometimes president. We have had many battles fought because of such people and their evil. But even if you conquer one, another usually pops up promising many things sounding good and right until they get into power. And then it is what is good and right for them. And the people suffer."

"The High Scribe is one such as that on my world. And it is time to make a change in our political structure."

"It goes way beyond some political or idealistic agenda. He is guilty of murder. He killed Sarangerel."

"This is something this small circle has suspected for a long time. However, can you prove this to the rest of the High Council?"

"I was somehow able to be present and saw it as it occurred those many years ago. I do not know if there is any tangible proof in existence. It seems I am the only one who has the ability to put myself in that particular time and location to see it. I doubt if your High Council will take the word of a human against the High Scribe."

"No. It is not likely. But maybe there is still a way.

First, we must get—'Jack', as you call him, free of his current circumstances."

"Then you know where he is?"

"I believe I do. But it will not be an easy task and we will need some help. Especially once we are able to secure his safe return."

*

With the two ships docked and camouflaged, Brian and the old Gun Maker made their way into the disguised building containing the lab and workshop of the one Brian had given the name, Frank.

John met them and greeted them, explaining that his father was in his private workshop finishing with some important experiments and could not be disturbed.

"He is always working on something important and cannot be disturbed," the ancient non-Jack said. "I believe he just likes to be alone and revisits his past lives."

"He is spending more time than usual in his private workshop. No one else ever goes in. He will not even allow me inside or share any information about his projects and he blocks any communication in." said John.

"What happens if there is an emergency or a problem only he can take care of," Brian asked?

"Even with all communication blocked, he somehow knows," John returned.

Just to prove the point somehow, Frank emerged from his private workshop.

Brian closed his eyes for a second to the high-pitched screeching going through his brain emanating from Frank that must have been the old Gun Maker's non-Jack name. There was no attempt to keep the conversation between the two, private.

Frank walked over to him and put a hand (foot?) on the side of his old and wrinkled triangular face.

"My old mentor has come to see me after all these cycles. Are you here to check on me or are you here to steal my secrets?"

"*Your* secrets?" Declared the ancient Gun Maker. "You are the one who used the knowledge I shared with you for your own purpose. Look what it has cost you. Exiled to this, this—"

"It is my home."

"And you are still conducting your unauthorized experiments."

"As you have said, you shared the knowledge with me. I was not going to just let it die. There was much to prove and much to change."

"And later, many questioned whether you were the right one to put into the position of Gun Maker."

"Did you question your decision to make me your apprentice?"

"I question everything. However, with you, that was

never the situation. You were always my choice."

"I was not the only choice?"

"No. There were several others. All showed promise. You displayed something special. Something different. I knew you were the only one who was meant for the position. You made it yours. I believe one day, you will have it back."

"I am doing just what I want to do here. I am not so sure I want it back. Or that the Council would want me back. Remember, with the demands of the High Scribe, they are the ones who forced me out. There are too many on the Council the High Scribe controls."

"This is not where you belong. You are in exile. In hiding. Not even on the world of your self-awareness. You are the Gun Maker. There is no other who can do what you do. The position is yours. Fight for it. The knowledge is yours. Use it. There is none other."

"There is yourself."

"That is not an option. My time has passed."

"And even if I did want to stop hiding, just how am I supposed to win over the Guardian of The People and have the Council welcome me back?"

"You start by giving them this human.

PART THREE

William N. Gilmore

CHAPTER 26

Brian was standing in front of the Council. He couldn't see them or hear their thoughts. The special contraption he wore on his head kept him from that. It was something Frank made to fit his human head. In fact, Frank was the one who brought him before the Council. As he did, he bowed deeply.

Brian also wore a device securing his hands behind his back. He was more than just a prisoner. He was being offered as a tribute to both the Council and the High Scribe from Frank.

Frank made the arrangements through another home-world scientist to surrender Brian. There were several conditions; to include allowing Frank to come out of exile to make the delivery himself. Furthermore, any negotiations they may enter into, whatever the outcome, would include the safe and undisturbed passage of Frank and his party. The Council agreed. The High Scribe grudgingly accepted the terms as well but insisted Brian would not be allowed to have any voice in any proceedings. He was only a lowly human. However, Frank and Brian knew the High Scribe had his own reasons for keeping him silent.

"I bring you this human," Frank began, "as a show of good faith in my belief in The People and our way of life. The human, inferior as he is, did show some abilities when he came to me for asylum. However, he is human after all and is dangerous. Although I tolerate the humans I know, and I see some benefit from them, I believe it would be best to have them returned to their world or to have them put into permanent stasis. This is our world, our People, and we should maintain its purity."

"And just what has caused you to come to this belief, ex-Gun Maker?" the High Scribe asked as he maneuvered his small disk around the great hall. "It is well known of your fondness for these creatures."

Many of the Council showed their agreement with the question and awaited a qualifying answer.

"This has always been my belief. I am a scientist. The humans are merely a curiosity and are easily manipulated. A few have shown limited abilities. Their very existence is bewildering. I only wished to experiment to broaden our understanding, and to see if they could be enhanced to be more useful to us."

"Your experiments have gone too far," demanded the High Scribe as he floated just a few feet from Frank.

"You have defied the Council. You have created things beyond the scope of good science."

"Yes," continued the ex-Gun Maker. "Such is the nature of experimenting. However, I fully admit now to the Council that I have intentionally created things that are unacceptable. I now understand my wrongs. I have since destroyed the creations of my experiments and I have destroyed my lab. I only wish to return to the place of my first awareness and to be of service to the Council and to The People once again. I start by bringing you this despicable and unworthy human who has created a disturbance in the balance of our world."

There was a frenzy of communications between the members of the council. It continued a short while until the Guardian of The People silenced all of the members on the Council. The silence, or rather, the rare lack of any telepathic communication between the non-Jacks lasting only a short time, was almost disturbing until the Guardian of The People sent his powerful thoughts.

"The High Scribe has provided evidence that this human is dangerous. It may be inherently so with all humans. Although it may have been right to protect and continue the species, it was wrong to have them incorporated into our society. As Guardian of The People, it is ordered that this human be placed into stasis until he and the rest of the humans can be returned to their world. The ex-Gun Maker has shown great service to The People and I would ask the Council to reverse the order of exile and return the Gun Maker to his position on the Council."

The High Scribe immediately moved to a position in front of the Guardian of The People.

"May I remind the Guardian of The People and the Council that the now ex-Gun Maker refused to obey the past orders of the entire Council with regards to those experiments," the High Scribe protested.

"And may I remind The High Scribe that you are just one member of the Council and a vote of the entire Council is in order for his reinstatement. Moreover, although others have attempted to gain the position, primarily under your direction and have not survived, there is currently not a fully experienced Gun Maker on the Council."

"I apologize to the Guardian of The People and the Council," the High Scribe said with a bow of his triangular head. "It is only my intent to be of service and to provide the best I can for The People."

"As we all know. As my advisor, it is important the Council continues to look to you for your strength and guidance as we see to the future of our world and The People."

It took all the High Scribe's inner power to conceal his emotions and real thoughts towards the Guardian of The People and the apparent soon to be reinstated Gun Maker.

CHAPTER 27

Brian was roughly led out to a platform and placed onto a transportation disk. The disk traveled only a short while before arriving at another platform where he was pulled down. He was led into a huge structure where he was made to kneel.

The device on Brian's head was being removed and when it was off, his eyes began to adjust to the light once more. There was a non-Jack guard on each side of him as well as another off towards what appeared to be a control center.

He could see he was in a vast tube-like structure where there were capsules lining the entire circle of wall space. The wall space appeared to go on forever, up and down. There must have been thousands, maybe tens of thousands of capsules lining the walls.

This must be the area where The People and humans were placed into stasis. Brian was amazed at the number of capsules. Each containing a being.

The non-Jack guard at the control center made some adjustments and soon, a panel in the floor opened and a capsule arose through the opening. It came to a stop just feet from Brian and his other guards. A door on the capsule opened with a hiss as the air seal was cracked. One of the guards pointed at the capsule indicating Brian was to get in. Brian, having protected his thoughts ever since the device was taken off his head, now sent a single thought that was picked up by the device securing his hands. The specially made shackles opened and fell to the floor with a clang.

All three of the guards were so bewildered they failed to move quickly and did not notice the arrival of the old Gun Maker and Frank. They also didn't react to the distinctive crackling sound, not knowing what was coming. They made easy targets.

Frank went over to the guard at the control center while the ex-Gun Maker wrapped the arms and legs of the other two guards around each other and placed the special shackles on them. Without the special telepathic code to unlock them, they would find themselves together for a very long time.

Frank used the thought control device of the weapon on the remaining guard. Once under Frank's control, he instructed him to retrieve a specific capsule.

The door of the capsule on the platform closed and retreated into the open panel and disappeared. After a few moments, another capsule rose in its place.

The little guard, still under Frank's influence, manipulated more of the controls, and soon the door on the capsule popped open, releasing a thick cloud of fog, surrounding it. Frank gave the guard one final command before shooting him once more.

As the hazy fog around the capsule slowly began to clear, Brian and Frank saw the ancient Gun Maker carrying Jack's limp form out of the mist.

"Is he alive?" Brian weakly asked with concern for his friend as they boarded the waiting disk.

"Yes," answered the old Gun Maker. "It is only the effect of being in stasis. He will shortly return to normal. We must hurry though before we are discovered."

Brian and Jack were covered by a tarp of the strange material to conceal them. The disk silently sped towards the destination projected to it.

"It will not be long before the High Scribe is aware of our involvement with the escape of the human," the old Gun Maker stated.

"No," returned Frank, "But he will be very busy with other matters and maybe the delay will permit our own escape."

"What matters would he find more important?"

"I instructed the guard to release all the others who were placed in stasis, starting with the ones who had been ordered there by the High Scribe himself."

"I see I have taught you well."

The disk arrived at a destination far from the eyes and minds of anyone searching for them. The cover was thrown off Brian and Jack. They had arrived at the far cliffs and waterfalls of the home of the creatures Sarangerel called Hiimori.

"I am grateful for the rescue," Jack sent the weak thought. "I hope there were no problems."

"No, there were no problems," returned Frank. "In fact, I thought it was quite enjoyable."

"Although we have confidence in Brian's enhanced abilities," the old Gun Maker added, "we made sure he had full protection from the probes of the High Scribe, the Guardian of The People, and the rest of the council."

"That was probably wise," Jack returned. "I doubt many of us could withstand the combined efforts of all of them. Why are we at this location?" he inquired, his strength slowly returning by evidence he was now standing without help.

"We thought this would be a good place to meet with the rest of our party and continue our strategy," stated the old Gun Maker.

"Much has happened since I last saw you, my friend," Brian smiled. "When you are better we will tell you what has transpired. Right now, we need to make sure we—"

A loud roaring noise distracted them as they saw the flying Pegasus scatter from their playful acrobatics over the river and cliffs. A disturbance began in the middle of the widest part of the honey-colored river. Before long, the liquid began to bubble and spout. It continued for a few seconds before a structure was observed rising above the surface of the ancient alien tributary. As it continued to rise, its form became recognizable. It was the Hiimori. It cleared the river's surface, rising above the cliffs and landed on a level area not far from the disk holding the group.

The disk then maneuvered the short distance to the opened doors of the shuttle bay and entered the larger craft.

Once the transportation disk was secured, its occupants made their way to the control room. There on the bridge of the Hiimori was John.

"I see the operation was a success," John said with a little hint of a smile. He went over to Jack and showing respect and friendship, placed a hand (foot?) alongside his head. "I wish I could have seen that."

"You should have witnessed the guard's reactions when Brian dropped the special restraints that he suggested, and I made," Frank sent. "It was a strange human invention I was told."

"Actually," Brian laughed, "it was from a trick performed by a human named Houdini. Only instead of a real hidden key, Frank constructed it with a control that allowed for me to think it open once the helmet was removed just before I was to be placed into stasis. That set up the distraction allowing Frank and the elder Gun Maker to act and take control of the guards. However, it was all Frank's idea to get the guard to release the others from stasis. That was brilliant."

"And after I dropped Frank and Brian off at the Council

Hall, I made my way here and was submerged awaiting your arrival," John said. "Everything else is in place and others are waiting as requested."

"Let us be on our way then," Frank stated. "There is still much to do, and no one will be safe until we finish what we have started."

The Hiimori lifted off the surface and headed for its next destination with John still at the controls.

CHAPTER 28

Brian finally got Jack to himself for a few moments and gave him some personal updates.

"I saw him do it," Brian said, not trying to soften the terrible news he had for Jack. "Somehow I was able to finally make myself present during the High Scribe's murder of Sarangerel. There was an argument between them over your relationship. He threatened to send you away and put her in stasis along with the rest of the humans. She tried to defend herself and tried to use her gun. He threw a table just as she fired her weapon. That is why he must use a disk to get around. She disintegrated his legs. The table hit her in the head and she died instantly. However, I don't know if this record is available to be viewed by the Council and the Guardian of The People."

"We will make it so all of The People will be able to see what he has done," Jack said. A little sadness could just be detected in his thoughts. A lot of anger was there as well.

"I'm not sure how that is possible. I don't even know how I was able to see it."

"I do," Jack said. "It came from within you. I knew you were the one."

"The one what?" Brian asked.

177

"Every so often on your world," Jack began, "there are a few humans who are born with abilities beyond normal human capabilities. The abilities lie dormant for many years and sometimes they develop with age. Sometimes the abilities come along too soon and cause damage to the brain. This causes humans to be born with or develop abnormalities. Sometimes they are barely able to function and sometimes death. Many of the humans you refer to as savants are such. Humans with extraordinary insight, or what you call a sixth sense and those who are able to tell fortunes and read minds. Even fewer have developed the power to move objects using only their thoughts."

"So, why did you choose me?" Brian asked. "I never had any real abilities and I am definitely no savant. Yeah, I had hunches and feelings about certain cases, or I knew I was on the right track when others went in other directions, but I couldn't read minds or make people act in a certain way. I'm nothing special."

"You are wrong, Brian. You, my friend, are among those extraordinary humans. I saw the potential. Your abilities are the most powerful I have ever felt. Although they have just recently emerged, they are still expanding. The training I gave you has little to do with the abilities themselves, but how to focus them; how to cope with them. Everything you are able to do comes from within yourself. It was because of this and the person you are that I chose you."

"To find Sarangerel's murderer," Brian said matter-of-factly.

"I already knew for myself the High Scribe was responsible. I knew what his ultimate fate must be."

"So, you used me. Was I bait or a distraction? Did you bring me here to kill him for you as your own revenge?"

"None of that. I need you to help me prove to the Council that he is not who he pretends. Your abilities have now exceeded my own. Only you will have the power to stand up to him. You can help save my world from the destructive path he has set into motion."

Jack began to wobble a bit and Brian grabbed him before he fell.

"You are still weak from being in stasis," Brian cautioned.

"Yes, but it is more than that. Due to the interrogation, I need to rejuvenate sooner than I anticipated, or I will continue to weaken until I am dead. However, I don't think I will be welcomed into the city to do so."

"Surely there is somewhere else that you can do that. There must be other locations that you can make contact with the spires."

"No. That is why the city was built where it is. That is the only source of rejuvenation on the planet."

"Then that is what we must do. We will get you to the

spires," Brian promised.

Brian gave the bad news to the rest of the rag-tag group about Jack's need for rejuvenation sooner than was anticipated. There was much discussion about how to go about getting this done, but no solution.

Frank and John knew the consequences of not rejuvenating and didn't bring up that part of the problem, although Frank stated he wouldn't need rejuvenating for many more cycles, or several hundred years in human terms.

John, being a hybrid, wasn't even sure if he would ever need to make contact with the spires. If he ever started feeling that he did, he wasn't sure if he would be allowed to either. He didn't like the idea of testing it too soon.

The Hiimori continued its predetermined path through space. Jack was resting while Frank and John went over their next move. Brian was still contemplating what Jack told him. As he sat in one of the chairs fabricated for his human form, he stared at all the stars and wonders of the universe in front of him. He felt a deep longing. A sadness overcame him. He closed his eyes.

CHAPTER 29

Brian found himself speeding down a country road with trees, fence posts, and cows going by at an alarming rate. Slowly they started to come into a normal perspective and before long, it turned into a delightful afternoon drive. The sun was shining, and the temperature was mild while the cool breeze coming in through the open windows carried a fresh cut grass smell that was more than pleasant.

He looked over to the passenger seat and Angie wore a cute, floppy, straw hat with a big, colorful band; its tails flowing in the wind. She had on overly large tortoiseshell sunglasses and hung her well-tanned arm out the window. Her hand knifed out to catch the flow of the air like an airplane's wing, forcing her arm up and down as she angled it. She laughed.

Brian laughed as well. He was happy. Something that had escaped him for a very long time. He reached over and took Angie's other hand in his. She turned and smiled, mouthing the words 'I love you' to him. It was a beautifully perfect day.

The squealing of tires as a speeding truck on a cross street failed to stop in time at a stop sign brought Brian back to reality. This is where the dreams and nightmares usually ended. Sometimes though, not until after the awful screams, the crash, and the tearing of metal and breaking glass. And then there were the far-off sirens. Brian was still holding Angie's hand as he fell into the darkness.

Brian woke from his coma in the hospital a week later. He learned Angie never made it that far. The nightmares started shortly after.

A heavy shuddering of the ship brought Brian out of his troubled slumber.

"We are under attack!" John said. "There is another ship firing at us."

"Who is it?" Brian asked, while everyone else scrambled for their own seats and strapped in.

"It must be the Devorex," Frank sent. "They are the only ones close to this sector who have space flight and energy weapons. They are a highly-advanced society, but lacking the ability for telepathic communication, they are hard to reason with and just a little too aggressive."

"But why are they firing at us?" Brian questioned. "What do they want? Are you at war with them?"

"Nothing like that," the old Gun Maker tried to explain. "I think it's me they want. I exchanged some technology with them through an intermediary. I tried to emphasize the importance of how dangerous it was, but they wouldn't listen. I understand it destroyed most of one of their moons."

The ship rocked again but sustained no damage.

"Shouldn't we be firing back," Brian suggested.

"They are just trying to get our attention. Maybe stop and talk. They may even want to exchange more technology," the past Gun Maker sent out, trying to reassure everyone. "We should stop and see what they want."

"But they are firing on us," Brian reiterated.

"Yes, but just with their minor weapons. If they really wanted to destroy us, they would have done so already."

As the ship slowed and soon came to a stop, the Devorex ship passed over the Hiimori, blocking out the stars above. Brian watched as the ship, dark and ominous, continued to shadow their own and soon, the size of the other alien ship was beyond belief. The ship must have stretched on for miles before it too came to a stop just above the Hiimori.

The old Gun Maker was obviously quite taken aback as well. "I don't recall the Devorex having a ship like this. Surely not one of this size anyway."

Doors opened in the belly of the ship and the Hiimori gave a slight jerk and began to be pulled into the other ship by some force. Brian ran over to where his weapons were stored, but Frank countered the move and told him not to arm himself. That any suggestion of aggression on their part could be misinterpreted and would be met with possible deadly force. The Devorex would not give them a second chance.

Some type of clamps or securing mechanism grabbed the

Hiimori which was now fully inside the Devorex ship and the alien ship's bay doors closed.

"Now what?" Brian continued with the questions. "Who are these guys?"

"We wait," the ex-Gun Maker returned. "It's part of their way of telling us they are in control."

"You've dealt with them before, so tell us what to expect."

"I am not sure what to expect. My experience with them is limited. However, I can tell you they are not like you or me. They come from a far-off system with double yellow suns. It is rare to see them out this far. They live on a large, mostly desert planet with nearly 400 moons. They are what your world would consider reptilian in appearance. They have scales, walk on two feet and have two arms. They have two sets of eyes, one set forward and the other to the sides of their head that can look behind them. They breathe air much as we do, but I believe they have the ability to not breathe for long periods. Somewhere along their early evolution, they became smart and progressed fast.

"So, what you are telling me is that we are now being held against our will inside a spaceship filled with aggressive and overly smart alien alligators you may have pissed off at one time."

"Something like that," the old Gun Maker conceded.

CHAPTER 30

Several hours passed while everyone waited to see what the Devorex would do next. Surely, they were not captured by them just to be destroyed now. And Brian was starting to get the feeling again that he might be someone's meal.

"Tell me more about these Devorex and what exactly was your involvement with them," Brian demanded of the former Gun Maker

"There are several divisions or cliques within their society. And among these are a number of factions. There are warriors and traders. Explorers and scientists. All of them fighting to gain control over the other and each surviving because of the resources provided by the other. It is a constant conflict of ideals, loyalties, and power."

"It is a wonder how they have been able to survive, much less progress to a point where they have an advanced civilization that includes space flight," Brian relayed. "And how did you come to be tangled up in their little part of the universe?"

"I learned through a third party about a mineral on one of their moons containing certain properties I needed for my experiments. A trade was arranged, but I needed to give a demonstration of my product. I met with one of their representatives and I got to know something about their world and communication, which is really a series of clicks more than speech. I was able to quickly pick it up and—"

Brian jumped in. "What exactly was your product to be traded, again?"

"I did not say. It was just some technology to help them with advanced research."

"Something a Gun Maker might know?"

"A Gun Maker has knowledge of many things."

"Okay, I understand you don't want to tell me. Continue with your story."

"As I was relating, I learned to communicate with them. I spent several cycles there. Unfortunately, their lifespan is rather short, and I worked with several generations of the same family until I believed they possessed the working understanding of— well, the technology, and I was able to acquire enough of their special mineral for my own projects."

"You mentioned something about one of their moons being destroyed?"

"It was not completely destroyed. And it was a small moon at that. Uninhabited and barren. They were the ones who went beyond the recommended settings. I gave them plenty of warnings."

"So, it really was a type of weapon you gave them," Brian sent with a tone of disgust. "And now I learn you are an interplanetary arms dealer. No wonder they want you. Is there a price on your head or do they just want revenge?"

There was a pounding at the airlock hatch of the Hiimori and then a very audible series of clicks that seemed to come from everywhere.

"They want us to open the hatch," the old Gun Maker relayed the translation. "And it was not a request."

John gave a signal that pressure was now equalized between the Hiimori and the outside, allowing Frank to open the airlock hatch to a very bright light and a stale and pungent odor. Brian still held his breath and shut his eyes tight as if the alien air was a poisonous gas or contained harmful biological elements. When he couldn't hold it any longer, he slowly began to exhale and opened his eyes, blinking several times. This was not the soft rose hue of Jack's world.

Brian took a second to adjust and focus but still gasped upon seeing several of the Devorex at the airlock. He began coughing violently, involuntarily backing up a few steps. Nothing Frank could have told him prepared him for the sight before him now.

What Brian saw would not exactly fit a description of alien alligators. Yes, they displayed dark scales on their face and on their bodies that weren't covered by what looked like military style clothing. They carried short, misshapen tubes in a way that they may have been weapons.

They also had a slightly protruding snout showing some pretty mean teeth. There were two sets of eyes just as the ex-Gun Maker described and they even walked on two feet and had two arms. However, the most noticeable thing about them was not their facial appearance, nor the fact they were missing a tail, but that they were only about two feet tall. Much smaller than even Frank or Jack.

If their arms had been shorter and their snouts longer, they may have almost passed for a child's toy dinosaur. But it was more than a child's toy pointing a strange looking non-toy weapon at them. They were real. The tube weapons brought on a feeling that wasn't too funny.

A series of clicks came from one of the creatures in the doorway and the ancient Gun Maker returned his own audible response.

"We are to follow them to a waiting area. Any resistance and they will shoot," the Gun Maker translated. "I told them we would not resist and that we are on a peaceful mission."

"Great," Brian said. "More waiting. And are those the weapons you made for them?"

"No, those are not of my design. They may be functional, but the workmanship lacks a personal touch."

"Well, do you have any idea yet what they have planned for us?"

"No. This is just a greeting party," the old Gun Maker

stated as they all began to exit their ship and continue down a ramp. "Someone in authority will meet with us soon."

"Greeting party? Not much of a greeting with guns pointed at us and I don't see any balloons or cake for a party. I will say that this was not what I was expecting."

"Were you hoping for something more female, blonde and exotic."

"Not necessarily, but I did expect something taller."

"And is that what you thought when you first encountered us?" Frank asked.

"You were the first aliens I ever met. I didn't have any real expectations before that," Brian tried to explain. "I still don't. From telepathic explorers and hybrids to shapeless blobs that produce an edible by-product to flying horses and now this. I will keep my mind open to whatever may come next."

"That is always a good idea," Jack threw in. "This is just a small section of the vast universe. You would not believe—"

Several of the greeting party took a big interest in John. They may never have seen a hybrid before now.

A quick series of sharp clicks came from what must have been the creature in charge of the Devorex greeting party.

They continued until their greeters stopped them at a panel that slid open once the lead Devorex gave an announcement. Although the door opening was much taller than the Devorex, Brian still had to duck to enter along with everyone else. The room was bare of any furniture or fixtures. The light was still bright.

The lead Devorex approached Brian and uttered a few clicks. Brian just stared at him. The lead Devorex then pointed his weapon at Brian and made a few more clicks.

Quickly the ex-Gun Maker made several clicks himself at the Devorex and one set of eyes went to the old Gun Maker while the other two were hard set on Brian. All the Devorex seem confused with eyes going back and forth from Frank to Brian to John.

One of the Devorex, with his weapon still out, came over to Brian and began to sniff him at his legs.

The prior Gun Maker made several long series of clicks and he and the head Devorex seemed to be in a disagreement over something. This continued for several minutes until the entire greeting party backed out of the doorway and the door came down.

"And what was that about?" Brian asked.

"They wanted to put you in a separate area. They thought you were my property and that I was bringing you here to trade."

"Why would they think that?" Brian questioned.

"Because they have been trading for humans with the High Scribe for many cycles.

CHAPTER 31

The waiting again was several Earth hours long already. No food or drink had been brought and the floor of the room made for bad comfort.

"Are we now prisoners of these little monsters?" Brian asked.

"I am not sure," the elder Gun Maker sent. "I don't know how close their association with the High Scribe might be and I am even questioning why they stopped us the way they did. Our worlds and our societies are so different, it is hard to understand their reasoning and motives."

"They seemed very interested in me," John finally spoke up for one of the few times. "I bet they never encountered anyone quite like me. I wonder why they didn't think I was your property as well."

"They may have been able to make the family connection somehow." Jack surmised. "They may have some ability we don't know about. Maybe hyper-sensitive smell or sight that allows them to distinguish the difference between things. But the less said, the better."

"True," Brian agreed. "And they could even have a hidden agenda. It's funny how you think you can learn about someone and then find they have secrets that changes your perspective. I mean, all of a sudden, I find there are interplanetary gunrunners and human slave traffickers right under my nose. I wonder what other dirty little secrets I'll find.? What else is this universe hiding? Don't you have any space police or galactic sheriffs who bring all the cosmic bad guys to justice?"

"Each society handles its own problems," Frank told Brian. "There is not a pact or agreement between systems. There is no universal law."

"And what about war?" Brian asked of Frank. "Are there planets or systems at war or threaten to go to war?"

"All the time. Some wars are eons old and it never looks like there is an end. Some wars have planets with many inhabitants destroyed or conquered. There are sure to be systems that have been conquered many times by many different races of beings and there are sure to be highly intelligent beings who are now extinct because of stupid wars. It has always been and it shall always be. It is the nature of things."

The door began to rise and as it did, they all got to their feet. There in front of them was a single Devorex, unarmed and wearing not military attire, but a flowing blue robe. He bowed, his head almost touching the floor. Several clicks were made before he straightened up and when he did, he made a series of several more.

The past Gun Maker turned to the rest of his group. "He apologizes for the delay and requests we accompany him for refreshments and conversation."

"Just who is he supposed to be?" John asked.

"He may be a diplomat," Jack guessed, "or, he may be the executioner."

"Either way, we will know soon enough," Brian stated. "I say let's go with him. I'm getting hungry and that floor isn't getting any softer."

The group followed the blue robed Devorex to a hall where there was a short table filled with food and drink.

Again, the Devorex diplomat bowed and made a few of the clicking sounds before exiting.

"He says to indulge yourself," the ex-Gun Maker quoted.

"I hope this isn't where they fatten us up before the kill," Brian said, but still tore into the food.

There was a cheese type substance and something like bread. Something Brian had not seen since leaving Earth. There were also some items reminding Brian of real fruit, not something from a blob's butt.

Frank and Jack just stood and watched as Brian literally made a pig of himself. John tested the fruit which he found very delicious.

"I doubt they would poison us at this point, however, I do not know their motive for this treatment," the ancient Gun Maker stated.

Brian stopped chewing just long enough to give the previous Gun Maker a disapproving look. What he actually thought should not be mentioned here.

When Brain was full, he sat on one of the padded benches that had been provided. He gave a very loud belch before politely excusing himself. It was almost like a picnic.

"That was really good. I almost hurt myself," Brian boasted. "The only thing that would have made it better is if they had some cream soda."

"I am sorry," Frank exclaimed. "Next time I'll be sure to have it ordered for you."

"Don't be upset with me, Frank. You have to remember that real food is something we humans crave and besides needing for our survival, enjoy."

"You are right. Again, I have failed to realize the narrow-mindedness and shortcomings of humans."

Just as the two minds were meeting to argue the point, the door opened and another Devorex walked in. This time, he was not alone, but with a column of members of the same race on either side of him, each wearing a different colored robe. He, himself was wearing a multi-colored robe. When they stopped, the columns bowed. The one in the middle did not.

There was a very fast, overly loud and long set of clicks from the one in the middle. Brian focused hard on the leader. Not for what he might be communicating but straining to enter deeper into the strange creature's mind. After a few laborious moments, Brian visualized a completely extra-terrestrial world. It was hot and very bright from the two yellow suns hanging high in a hazy sky. The land was a crusty desert with stone structures long ago crumbled to the ground. There were no inhabitants.

Brian began to sense something even stranger, darker in the mind of the alien. He saw cages filled with humans and then he saw the face of the High Scribe.

The former Gun Maker returned several clicks and appeared to be interrupted by the middle figure who clicked back at an even more furious pace and then turned and began walking out with the columns quickly pacing him.

Brian lost the vision of the dead world; the world that may have once been the home of the Devorex; the caged humans, and the High Scribe. He would keep this information to himself until he got a better understanding of what he saw.

The old Gun Maker turned and faced the others. "You were right Brian, I was wanted. But not for the reason you might think. They want me to make them weapons. They are planning on going to war.

CHAPTER 32

The group was taken to a much more comfortable room where there were cushioned couches and tables with the real fruit. If they were prisoners, then these were the best cells to have.

Jack was the first to speak up about the situation. "Surely there was more in what the Devorex said to you."

"They believe I was sent here by the High Scribe as part of a negotiation. The rest was between us," the ex-Gun Maker stated. "There will be no more discussion about it. I am the one they want. They want the Gun Maker."

"Then they do not know I am the current Gun Maker?" Frank asked.

"There is no reason for them to have that information," the old Gun Maker stated. "And no reason to give it to them."

"So, are you going to do as they ask? Are you going to make them weapons?" Frank demanded an answer.

"We will be in negotiations again soon. I need more information and the scope of the situation. I do not make weapons for just anyone to do as they please with them. And when I do make them, I do not make them without a price."

"What do you have with which to negotiate? Why should

they negotiate anything?"

"This is something I will need to handle. There is information I must obtain. You have other business to continue. It is important you succeed. Our world may depend on that outcome."

Blue Robe came into the room requesting the Gun Maker come with him.

While the old Gun Maker was gone, Brian told everyone else that he was able to get a glimpse into the mind of the lead Devorex. He saw their home planet and believed it was dead or dying from the results of war where they suffered immeasurable loss. That was why they wanted weapons. It was a fight for their survival.

"Is it possible that this ship contains the last of the Devorex?" John asked. "That this ship is their world now?"

"I do not see how that could be possible," Jack sent. "The Devorex numbers are extraordinary. I do not know of another race that has the technology and the numbers to cause this."

"Well," Brian began, "what about one that came from some other galaxy with conquering other worlds as its agenda. I mean, not long ago, I wasn't aware of you or any other civilizations other than my own world. How many worlds are out there with life, intelligent life, or conquering bands of aliens?"

"The possibilities are endless," Frank agreed. "There are many stories brought back to us from our explorers about other worlds and civilizations with the ability to travel in space. Some friendly, some not. Your world for example. Since our first encounter with your world, you have been able to expand your technology and enter the realms of space, limited as it might be so far."

"But the distance is so far," Brian exclaimed. "How far would someone go to make war with another species? And how would they have any knowledge of them in the first place?"

"We have learned to travel great distances and have what we believe to be superior intelligence, however, there may be civilizations much older and much more advanced than we are," Frank admitted.

"And hopefully wiser for it," Brian added. "It just seems a waste for a people to be too war like who have advanced to the point of having space travel."

"It might be why a civilization could survive so long," Frank speculated. "Being the superior force and continuing to advance in technology and adding to their conquests. It may be what the Devorex did and plans to continue."

"Like the Romans on my world," Brian recalled. "For many years, the Romans were the dominant force in almost every respect and attempted to put all the world under their rule, but they eventually were conquered themselves. It happened over and over again with some person or army trying to become my world's ruler and again and again, they were stopped by a determined group, an outside force, or they failed for some other reason."

"Yes, I remember how the Romans used their might and political structure to spread their empire to many far-off lands on your world," Frank conveyed. "They weakened their influence when they spread themselves out, making them more venerable."

"That's right," Brian said. "You were there on my world for a time. You lived some of our history. Did you happen to help make any?"

"Remind me sometime to tell you the story about my suggestion to the Pharaoh's architect for the building of several monuments and tombs."

"Are you saying you suggested the Great Pyramids?"

"Oh, so you have heard this story before?"

Brian sat with his mouth open for a short time but was interrupted by the entrance of the blue-robed Devorex.

The Devorex bowed and although the clicks he made were not translatable by anyone there, his motions showed they were to follow him.

The four followed the Devorex to a section of the large ship where there was what could be described as a tram or transportation module system. It was hovering over a single rail that went far into the ship in both directions.

The Devorex entered into a compartment of what looked like a Japanese bullet-train. The others boarded the craft, finding the space cramped due to their size, especially Brian. There were no seats, nor any visible controls.

The blue-robed Devorex entered last and voiced his clicking and a door closed before the craft began to move at a very quick pace with just the slightest movement perceived.

"I wonder where he is taking us," John sent to all the others. "I really don't like not knowing if we are guests or prisoners or something even worse."

"Brian, can you read anything in our escorts mind?" Frank asked. "Your abilities seem to allow you to make a defined mental connection where all I see is a fog."

"I'll see what I can do," Brian returned. He closed his eyes and concentrated on the Devorex. The alien mind was so different, even from Jack and his race, that he had to strain to focus as he did in the previous attempt on the leader. But this Devorex possessed other thoughts than about his desolated home. His thoughts were odd and terrifying. Thoughts of alien lust and hunger. Thoughts that were so disturbing, Brian started to shake. The strain was making Brian sweat and his knees became wobbly.

Frank and Jack grabbed Brian just before he was about to fall. There was no room for him to lie so they held him up the best they could. Luckily, the craft was coming to a stop. The Devorex seemed a bit unsteady himself, shaking his head before stepping out of the craft, almost falling face first on the platform.

The connection between Brian and the Devorex was severed and Brian quickly was able to steady himself. He didn't say anything about what he had seen in the Devorex's mind.

Blue Robe took them to a location that appeared to be a huge laboratory. Larger even than Franks. The senior Gun Maker was there. The Devorex bowed and left.

"It is good to see you again," the old Gun Maker sent. "I hope they have treated you well."

"It's not about the treatment we are receiving," Brian stated. "It's why are we here. You say they want you to make them weapons. To use against what enemy?"

"They would not say directly. There is still much we are in negotiations about. I am sure that will come out eventually."

"What if I were to tell you the weapons they want you to make are to be used against your own people."

Everyone stared at Brian.

"Not only is he conspiring with them," Brian continued, "but the High Scribe is the one who is orchestrating this movement. He has promised the Devorex not only your world but mine as well.

"What makes you think the High Scribe is conspiring with the Devorex to take over our worlds?" The ex-Gun Maker demanded. "What would be his motivation?"

"I was able to see into the mind of one of the Devorex. The High Scribe has been trading humans to them in exchange for the same minerals you have sought."

The former Gun Maker was taken aback. "That is not possible. These minerals are unique and used for a very specific purpose. He cannot possibly have the knowledge nor the ability to—to—complete this experiment."

"Not only that," Brian continued, "but he has convinced the Devorex that it was your people who caused the destruction of their world."

"First," Brian stated, "he would elevate himself to the high position of Guardian of The People and he would not need a Council. No one to disagree with or challenge him. He would give the Devorex all the humans, whom he despises. He craves power above everything else and will do whatever it takes to achieve it. In his own sick mind, this would be like a new Cleansing, but one that he would control."

"That would be impossible," Frank said. "The Council would never allow him to do that. He doesn't have the authority or the power."

"He plans on eliminating the Guardian of The People and the entire Council," Brian stated.

"And you saw this in just one of the Devorex?" The old Gun Maker asked.

"Yes, that is true, but I've felt this in all of them we have encountered. There is hope, a longing. There is no attempt in them to hide or to lie about the truth. And there is more I did not mention."

"And what would that be?"

"This is not just about a conquest for a new place to live. It is about a source of food. They are flesh eaters. There are thousands of them on this ship, possibly many more elsewhere, and they are all very hungry. I now know the real reason the High Scribe has so many humans in stasis."

PART FOUR

William N. Gilmore

CHAPTER 33

Jack was confused. "Your world is uninhabitable, or at least it was," he told Brian.

"That is the information that was given to the Council and then passed on to us," Brian agreed. "Where did that information originate? What if the information was false?"

"It came from the High Scribe. He said it came from other ships that communicated their findings before we arrived. That is possible because there are certain of our ships that have the ability to travel much faster than what we were able to do. Their crews are placed into a type of stasis much the way you were, and they are able to stand the strain and exposure of the speed and radiation generated by the black holes."

"That may be true, but has anyone communicated with anyone that actually saw my world after we left?"

"But why would the High Scribe lie about the condition of your world?" the senior Gun Maker questioned. "How would that benefit him?"

"I've been trying to come up with an answer myself and I think I have. Now that we know he has made deals with the Devorex, it makes perfect sense. The High Scribe will first use the new weapons and numbers of the Devorex to put himself into power on your world, creating a dictatorship and handing over all the humans to them. Then he will give the Devorex the location of Earth where they will have an easy time with the new technology taking over the planet and making it their own. They will then have a replenishing food supply to support their growing needs."

"That is a pretty wild speculation," the ex-Gun Maker said, "but knowing the High Scribe, I can see him doing just that."

"We do have several things in our favor though," Brian suggested.

"That I am not human is one of them," John said.

"Lucky for you," said Brian. But I'm not sure that matters. First, I don't think the High Scribe is aware we have encountered the Devorex, at least, I hope not. They believe we are here on orders of the High Scribe, so they may not contact him to tell him of our—meeting. Also, they are completely unaware that I, as a human, can see into their minds. I may not understand everything as strange as it can be, but it is an advantage. Another is that we have the expertise of two Gun Makers on our side and we may soon have access to their special weapons."

"But we are just five against thousands on a ship that is larger than some moons," John said. And even if we did get to our ship and somehow get away. They have weapons that will destroy us before we get further than a Qasborag can jump."

"A Qas…?" Brian tried to ask about the strange word.

"A Qasborag is a…it is like a rabbit," Jack explained.

"Okay, whatever," Brian said, shaking his head. "We have some things to work out. The first thing I need to do is get back to the Hiimori, get some of the weapons we have, and get the ship ready to leave in a hurry. I also need to see how they have it secured and how to get the bay doors open."

"I better go with you," Jack said. "As a human, they may not trust you, or they may not be able to resist taking a bite out of you."

Brian thought about going alone, however, Jack made a good point. Two good points.

Brian was about to ask the old Gun Maker to call out to Blue Robe and just realized something.

"You know, I have given an Earth name that I can pronounce to everyone else but you. I can't just call you the Gun Maker without getting a look from Frank or possibly exposing you somehow. And it might get confusing when things are hurried. How about I give you a name I can remember?"

"Very well. What name would you like me to use to ease your conscience from being so inferior?"

"Here we go again," Brian said aloud under his breath. "How about Paul? Short, sweet, and easy to remember."

"If that is what you wish, you may call me Paul."

"Thank you. Paul, would you please call Blue Robe in and explain to him that I need to go back to our ship to use the sanitation facilities."

"That may not work. If they do keep humans here on this ship, they may have facilities for those humans as well."

"If they do have facilities for humans here, I am sure they are neither sanitary nor anything I would want to visit. Insist Jack and I be allowed to go back to the ship."

Paul went to the entrance of the lab and found there were two Devorex guards. Both guards were wearing the military-style uniforms and were armed.

He told them they needed to speak to the one wearing the blue robe. They responded they would have him contacted and to wait in the lab. Before long, Blue Robe came to the lab. Paul questioned him about the guards and was assured they were just for the safety of he and his party. Paul felt a little easier when he was able to easily convince him Brian and Jack should go back to the ship, adding in the explanation he did not want his human exposed to any of the others on board and Jack was to bring back some equipment from the ship he would need in the lab. The only requirement Blue Robe insisted upon was that the human and Jack needed to have an escort.

Two other Devorex soldiers came to the lab and Blue Robe clicked instructions to them. They were to be the escorts for Brian and Jack. Both were armed with the strange looking tubes.

Along the route back to the Hiimori, the two alien escorts clicked. Brian was starting to understand a bit of the clicks this time, however, to get the grip on what was really happening, he got into the minds of his escort. From what Brian saw, although they were being allowed to go their ship, they would never be returning to the lab.

Brian relayed to Jack what he read in the escort's minds and told him to send the information back to Paul before they got too far away while he continued to probe for information from the scaly soldiers. He also was forming the early stages of a plan.

They took the transportation system back to where the Hiimori was docked and the two Devorex soldiers kept all their eyes on Brian and Jack, continuing to click back and forth to each other only stopping when one of the two clicked apparent instructions to the transportation pad.

As they approached the ship, Brian noticed a single windowed room that may have been the location of the controls for the bay. It was occupied by only one Devorex.

Their escort took them into the Hiimori just as Brian finalized his plan and sent it to Jack.

"That's pretty risky," Jack returned to Brian. "Do you have a secondary plan if this does not work? One that may not have us being served as dinner to the Devorex."

"It's going to work," Brian sent out with confidence and

just a touch of sarcasm.

Brian started towards one of the other rooms within the ship, opening a portal. One of the Devorex soldiers started clicking and following Brian.

"Oh, no you don't," Brian said out loud to the creature. "I go alone to do my business."

The Devorex showed his menacing teeth, began clicking rapidly and pointed the tube at Brian.

Brian pointed at himself then towards the room, then at the Devorex and towards the spot the Devorex stood. The symbolism was clear, yet the Devorex soldier was not going for it. Brian shook his head and then bowed and gave a wave of his hand to show the Devorex that he was now to proceed him into the room.

The Devorex went into the room through the portal and as soon as he was in the room, Brian closed the portal behind him. Without the ability or knowledge of the portals, the Devorex was trapped in the room.

The other Devorex soldier was so surprised, Jack easily disarmed him of the tube weapon and pinned him to the deck of the Hiimori.

Brian quickly closed the hatch of the Hiimori and went to where he stored his weapons. He retrieved the weapon Frank made for him and went over to the soldier on the deck.

"Let him up," Brian said. "Let's see just what this thing

will do."

Jack released the hold on the Devorex and quickly backed up. Brian set the controls and then aimed the weapon at the creature and pulled the configuration of triggers. The weapon crackled and a streak shot out hitting the Devorex. What happened next was unfortunate. The poor creature grabbed his head and began running in circles. Two of his eyes popped out. The scream was terrible.

Brian wasn't sure what the reaction of the strange weapon would be on these small creatures, but he didn't expect this. The Devorex kept running and screaming, finally running into a bulkhead of the ship, striking its head and going down like a rock. The creature's head split open and a greenish ooze that must have been its blood came pouring out.

"Alright, that is one down," Jack said matter-of-factly, "how about the other?"

"I had the controls set in the medium range," Brian said, wide-eyed at the sight on the deck. "I didn't mean for that to happen. I just wanted to see if I could control him."

"I think you might consider resetting the controls. Maybe a lower setting would be best to start with."

"You think he's dead?" Brian asked, almost remorseful.

"Do you read anything from him?"

"Nothing. It's totally blank."

"This is true, but I had a use for him. Now we have to

deal with the other one. I am sure he is very upset about now. We must be careful when we open the portal. He's still armed."

Jack went to the controls of the ship. "I can remove the air from the room. I do not know how long they can go without air though."

"No. It's too risky," Brian declared, not wanting another dead Devorex on his conscious. "However, can you pump something in?"

"Of course. What do you have in mind?"

"Can you turn the whole room into a stasis pod?"

"That is brilliant. Yes, that should work, and it is something that should not kill him."

"Let's hope not. We need to use him to get the others and the ship free."

"Let us hope you can find the right amount of adjustment on the thought disrupter as well."

"First things first. Let's put him to sleep."

CHAPTER 34

Jack made the modifications on the controls for turning the sealed room into its own stasis pod and they would check on their guest soon.

"We will need to get back to the others in the lab soon," Jack realized. "These two Devorex will be missed before long."

Brian agreed, stating, "That is one reason I need at least one of these Devorex to stay alive and be under our control. I need to get to the room across the bay. I believe it has the controls for clamps holding the ship and the bay doors."

"We will need to have the others with us before we try that. If we are discovered before they are safely back here, we may have to fight the Devorex there and back. A fight we may not win or losses we cannot afford."

"Yes, you are right. Let's see how our little friend is getting along now and then we will have a better idea how to proceed."

Both Brian and Jack armed themselves and stood on either side of the entrance to the room. Brian opened the portal but with just a very small opening. Nothing happened. He opened it just a bit more and took a quick peek, pulling his head back quickly just in case he got fired at. Again, nothing happened. He saw the Devorex soldier lying on the deck. He took a longer look, opened the portal all the way and then stepped into the room, ready to fire if the Devorex moved. He didn't.

Jack followed Brian into the room. Brian went over to the Devorex and relieved him of his tube weapon. Then he checked to make sure he was still alive. Not only did he check to see if the creature was breathing, which he was, but Brian also went into the unconscious being's mind. This Devorex soldier had a lot of lust in his inferior brain. Lust for another, or rather, several Devorex females as well as a craving for the flesh of certain non-Devorex beings. Especially one infuriating human. Brian quickly exited out of the vile thoughts of the Devorex.

"He's alive," Brian sent with obvious disgust. "He is dreaming."

"Good," Jack said. "The effects of the stasis should wear off quickly. Are you ready to try the thought disrupter again? Do you think you have the power at the correct setting?"

"I hope so. The minds of these soldiers are fairly simple. They represent the lower end of the scale of their species with basic instincts at the forefront; such as reproduction, food, and survival. They are easily manipulated by their superiors. Blue Robe and the leader are more complex. It's easy to see the hierarchy."

"Do you think you will be able to communicate with him

once he awakens?"

"I think so. I seem to have been able to pick up some of their language. I don't know if I got help from Paul or if it may be from being in their minds. Maybe a combination of both. I think I have a plan to get the other's attention really quick."

"That is good. I think I see him moving a bit. Let the fogginess wear off before you use it though."

Brian entered the room with his weapon pointed at the Devorex. He made a few clicks, waiting a few seconds for the situation to sink into the creatures limited brain, then repeating them again for the soldier's benefit.

The Devorex clicked back. An understanding was reached.

"What are you telling him?" Jack asked.

"That I wasn't going to harm him as long as he cooperated. I think I have to reinforce that thought though."

Brian made a few clicks at the Devorex and the creature slowly stood. He came to the edge of the open portal and saw his companion laying on the deck of the ship.

Brian made a few clicks and then aimed his weapon at the dead creature. Brian pulled the triggers and the Devorex soldier on the deck disintegrated before their eyes, uniform and all. It must have been organic material as well.

The remaining Devorex soldier took a step back. What might be considered a gasp and then a high squeal came from that alien mouth. Obviously shaken, his eyes were going wildly around until all four focused on Brian.

Brian made a few clicks and the lone soldier returned with a few slow clicks himself.

"What was said that time?" Jack asked.

"I told him his companion did not cooperate. He assured me he would."

Jack returned the room back to its previous condition. The Devorex soldier was left in the room for the time being until Brian and Jack could come up with more strategy. They took the rest of the weapons from a storage area and sorted them out. Brian had his Earth weapon and his special, custom-made weapon on his side. Jack had several of the weapons made by Frank for his group.

"I wonder what this tube weapon does," John inquired. "If they have these, what kind of weapons do they want Frank to make? Apparently, it will not shoot through the walls of this ship, or our friend, finding himself in the room with no way out, would have already tried that."

"It is a strange looking thing," Brian returned. "Does it shoot a projectile or a beam or does it have some other purpose?"

"We have two options. We can try to make it work ourselves and that could be very dangerous, or probably the better option is, we ask our guest."

"I vote for door number two," Brian quipped. "I have

several other questions for which I need answers before we make our way back to the lab. I think I'll be able to tell if he is lying or not."

"Are you not going to use the thought disrupter on the soldier?" Jack asked.

"I think seeing his dead buddy disappear was a pretty good thought disrupter. I just want to be cautious. I need this one alive. I will set the thought disrupter on its lowest setting and see if that will have the effect we need. If it kills him or fries his brain, we will have a heck of a time trying to get to the others and then back to the ship, much less, getting out of the belly of the whale."

Brian opened the portal to the room where the little Devorex sat on the deck. He was still shaken from the incident with his fellow soldier.

Brian clicked questions at the creature and received answering clicks back that Brian determined were truthful. The Devorex was not about to be any type of hero or deliberately give any false information. He saw what happens with lack of cooperation.

Brian went back and retrieved the tube weapon and clicked at the Devorex once more. A short series of clicks followed, and Brian laughed.

"What is that all about," Jack inquired. "What is so funny?"

"Guess what this weapon does?" Brian snickered.

"I would hope that you would tell me so that we may hurry with our plans," said Jack impatiently.

"Our little friend says it shoots a web out. It is used to capture things. It is non-lethal."

"The web may not be, however, once they capture you, then what are they going to do with you?"

"I see your point," Brian agreed. "That's not so funny. Okay, let's see if the thought disrupter is set properly."

Brian pulled the weapon once more and the little Devorex soldier squealed once more and tried to get as far away from Brian as he could. Brian quickly began clicking at the creature while adjusting the settings on the weapon.

Although Brian was trying to reassure the Devorex he was just going to stun him, the poor soldier was begging not to be disintegrated. Brian aimed and fired. The weapon crackled and a bolt reached out and struck the tiny creature right in the chest. His head didn't explode nor did it catch on fire. All four eyes were still in his head and were set as if looking off to a faraway galaxy.

Brian holstered the weapon and approached the soldier, beginning a series of clicks. As he did, he reached into the alien's mind and planted scenes to reinforce the instructions he was giving. Brian backed away and after just a short time the Devorex shook his head and clicked to Brian he was ready to escort them back to the lab.

*

Brian gave the tube weapon back to their soldier minion so as to not have it look suspicious to have him escorting them without it. Brian placed their weapons into a backpack with his things in storage. They took the transport back to the lab. Now the real test began.

Upon entering the lab, they found Blue Robe there with Paul, Frank, and John. Blue Robe appeared surprised to see Brian and Jack. He began a series of clicks with the escort away from Paul, unaware Brian had quickly learned their language or that the soldier was now under Brian's influence.

The Devorex soldier and Blue Robe clicked back and forth for a bit and Blue Robe seemed satisfied with the soldier's actions.

Blue Robe then went over to Paul, bowed and excused himself advising he had other duties to perform. He then exited the lab.

Paul immediately wanted to know what was going on and why it took so long for them to get back.

Both Brian and Jack explained in turns to all their party about what happened on the Hiimori. Then they told them what was said between the soldier and Blue Robe.

Brian gave the soldier certain instructions if he were to be challenged about bringing them back to the lab and the absence of the other escort.

Brian relayed that the soldier had indeed been questioned by Blue Robe. The soldier, under Brian's instructions, told him that Brian was using the facilities for humans on the ship while Jack was gathering instruments. The soldiers were to bring back the collected items to the lab after they secured the two in the ship with their weapons. However, when the other escort soldier grabbed one of the devices and began examining it, there was a flash of light and the soldier disappeared along with the device. He believed that this information might need to be brought to the attention of Blue Robe before he took any other action and wanted to get further orders.

"That is some little adventure you had," Paul stated. "Now what are you going to do?"

"We are going to get the heck out of here," Brian gave the direct answer. "They are not the hospitable guest they would have us believe. We need to go now while we still have the advantage."

"I agree with him," Jack stated. "It is not safe for us to remain any longer nor should we provide them with any weapon technology."

"I assume you have a plan to get us off this ship," Frank jumped in.

"Yes," Brian agreed. "But we must leave now."

Everyone agreed. Brian and Jack passed out the weapons they brought back.

"Try not to use them if you can. I want to use our escort here to get us back to our own ship and then help get it released. However, if something goes wrong, we may have to fight our way off."

Brian clicked to the Devorex soldier and the group then began to leave the lab headed for the Hiimori, but not before Paul grabbed a bag from one of the tables.

"Just some things from the lab I put together that we may need later," he said as he caught up with the others.

A guard outside the lab seemed confused and started clicking at their escort. A hurried series of clicks commenced between the two. It was obvious there was high tension between them and as the clicking peaked to one constant sound, their small companion raised his tube weapon and shot the guard. A web, not unlike a spider's, came out and wrapped the guard in a cocoon, pinning him against the wall. The guard did not struggle or even move.

The little Devorex soldier clicked a few times at Brian.

Brian relayed the communication. "He says he never liked him anyway. The capture web will keep the guard alive but secure for a while, even so, he will be found before long. He wants me to shoot him with my weapon and make him disappear.

I'm not sure that is something I want to do."

"That is one solution," Jack said. "However, I do not think that you are able to take a life like that, even one like this, without psychological repercussions."

"I understand your reservations, but what can we do? Hide him? We need to hurry," John was saying when there was the crackling of Frank's weapon. He had shot the guard. The guard, as well as the web, was gone.

"Okay," Frank stated plainly, "that takes care of that situation and no one has to have a breakdown over it. It is time to go."

Everyone seemed stunned for a moment except for their escort. He was still amazed at the technology of the weapon but was already running down the corridor to the transportation device that would take them to the Hiimori. Soon everyone followed.

As they boarded one of the hovering trams from its platform, Brian turned to Frank. "Was that really necessary? Did you have to kill the creature? Couldn't we have just hidden him as John suggested or put him in the lab?"

"I made the decision for all of us. It was not something I enjoyed or took pleasure in. It was something that needed to be done. I did not want it weighing heavy on your conscience or waste any time discussing it. It is done, now let us continue on and hope we do not have to do it again."

"Are you planning to destroy or disable the Devorex ship?" Paul asked. "If not, what is there to keep them from going to your world at some point? Or mine, for that matter?"

"We did not give them the weapon technology they need to be successful with such a mission," Brian explained. "Without that knowledge or someone to provide them with it, they will not be able to proceed. That is why we must get all of us off this ship. I prefer not to destroy them. They are just trying to survive as any of us would. I cannot judge them for their way of life nor would I want to be the one to condemn their species to annihilation."

"And you are willing to take the chance they will never get that technology?" Paul questioned Brian.

"Until I have other evidence, it is what I must do."

"Is that your idea of justice?" Paul asked.

"This is more than just an individual on trial. We are dealing with so much more." Brian insisted.

"I recall someone once said something about justice being for the civilized," Jack said. "And what about revenge and punishment? Are not those for the ones who *really* want something done? Has this philosophy changed?"

"So, you are in disagreement with me, my friend?" Brian asked. "What would you like to see happen?"

"It is not that I am in disagreement," Jack continued. "I would like to see you not so conflicted. I understand your knowledge and perceptions have changed greatly since you left your world. There has been much for you to absorb. And maybe I am greatly to blame. I have allowed too much too fast."

"No. One thing you said is correct. I am conflicted. After being in the thoughts of so many others, I realize I am not just an individual in the universe anymore. I have felt in the minds of others; hopes, desires, fears, deceit, hate, and love, plus so much more. Things I did not dare let show in myself for such a long time. I guess I am the recipient of my own justice."

"Or is it your own personal revenge and punishment on yourself?"

"What are you talking about?"

"You blame yourself for the loss of your wife."

"How dare you? You don't know what you are talking about. It was an accident."

"Of course, it was. And that is what you have told yourself all these years. But you do not believe it. You think somehow you should have been able to prevent it, to see it coming, or at least, believing you should have died in the accident along with your wife."

Brian just stared. The thoughts he was having were too well guarded. There were no indications of anger or guilt. No regrets or remorse. No hate, no sorrow, no self-pity. Nothing.

Jack began to feel a twinge in his head. Something he had not felt in many years. Something his father did when he was not paying attention and used as a punishment. He put his ten-fingered hand up to his head and shook it a couple of times. He looked back at Brian with a curious stare. Brian had just the slightest smile on his face.

They arrived at their destination, exiting the tram and making their way to the Hiimori without any other contacts or incidents. Brian pointed out the windowed room where he believed the controls for the bay doors were housed. He had a plan to get the doors open.

The other item on his short list that could be a problem was how to keep them from firing on and recapturing or destroying the Hiimori. He was still working on the plan.

John and Jack went to the controls and readied the ship for when their escape was ready to be put into action while Brian conferred with Paul and Frank about how to get safely away from the Devorex ship.

The little Devorex soldier began clicking at the three of them, but he was being ignored. He tried to get their attention, but his size, along with his position within the group, gave him a disadvantage at being heard.

The little alien soldier maneuvered unnoticed between Brian and Paul. Without any further warning, he kicked Brian in the shin and then once again began his chorus of clicks.

Paul looked surprised and Brian just opened his mouth. Frank, not yet having the knowledge of the Devorex language was asking what was going on.

As they all looked down on the excitedly, clicking creature, Brian smiled. Their tiny ally was providing information that might just give them a way out.

CHAPTER 35

The entire group was amazed to learn the effects of the thought disruption lasted only a short time on the Devorex soldier. He was actually cooperating on his own accord without the influence of anyone. He was happy to assist them if they would just take him with them. He was deserting.

Brian and Paul discussed the plan their tiny friend suggested, and it seemed it might even be feasible. It was better than anything they had come up with.

They needed to hurry though, the timing was everything. Everyone had their part to play and if this was to be successful, they needed luck to be on their side as well.

Brian and the little soldier made their way to the bay door control room. Brian entered with his hands raised while his short, scaly friend pointed the tube weapon at him. The tiny soldier clicked at the two engineers in the control room and told one of them to go and get someone in authority and have them come to the prisoner's ship for he found the human trying to escape and there was another captured in their ship.

One of the Devorex engineers ran out of the control room heading to get help. As soon as he was gone, Brian put his hands down, pulling his special weapon from a concealed location and fired the thought disrupter at the engineer. He adjusted the setting just a little higher for the effects to last longer than they did on his companion. Luckily, it did not seem to damage the engineer. Brian clicked to the engineer some instructions and then he and his cohort returned to the Hiimori.

It wasn't long before Blue Robe came to their ship. He brought three other soldiers with him. As they entered, he saw the one who had been assigned as the escort pointing his weapon at the human. A long series of clicks were exchanged, and Blue Robe seemed rather pleased.

Brian understood his soldier was telling Blue Robe he caught the human trying to get the ship ready to leave along with one of the others. He captured the other, securing him in a room on the ship. He wanted to show Blue Robe the other prisoner along with technology he found. It would be of vital interest to the Devorex.

The other soldiers were told by Blue Robe to wait there and to watch the human prisoner.

Blue Robe followed the soldier escort to the sealed entrance to the room where the Devorex escort waved a hand, and a portal opened. Blue Robe was quite impressed with his soldier's ability unaware Brian was the one who opened the portal on a prearranged plan.

The defected Devorex soldier bowed to his previous blue-robed superior and allowed him to enter first. As soon as he entered the room, Brian closed the portal and he along with Paul and Frank, who came out from a hiding spot, shot the three unsuspecting and distracted guards. Two of the guards became as statues, the other disappeared with his tube weapon clanging on the deck.

"Oops, I forgot to reset my weapon," Frank said apologetically. Brian gave him a scornful look, not believing a Gun Maker would forget something so simple. He gave the others instructions to turn over their weapons and to sit on the deck and not to move until told to do so. They quickly obeyed.

Brian went and opened the portal but did not allow their blue-robed prisoner out of the room. Instead, he and Paul went in. The little diplomat was confused, clicking for an explanation and then calling for his guards. He stopped clicking when Brian raised his weapon at him.

Brian demanded information on the relationship between the High Scribe and the Devorex. Blue Robe refused to answer. Brian told him he would give him one more chance to answer. There was silence from the Devorex representative.

"I really hate to do this," Brian said to Paul, "but bring in one of the soldiers."

Paul retrieved one of the emissary's guards, bringing him into the room with his weapon on the soldier. The poor Devorex was oblivious to his predicament. Brian told Blue Robe once again to give him the information he desired or this time his soldier would pay the price. There was only silence, but Brian could see in the alien mind of Blue Robe and could sense losing his soldier would be a great misfortune. He could see the hurt and frustration, yet he could also see the determination of Blue Robe not to divulge any information. The life of a mere soldier was a sacrifice he would have to deal with before giving up any information.

"Then we have no choice," Brian clicked. He turned and fired his weapon at Blue Robe. The weapon crackled, and the following streak hit Blue Robe in his small chest.

The diplomat was now very eager to provide the information Brian wanted when he asked again.

"Why didn't you just shoot him in the first place," Paul asked, "instead of trying to coerce the information out of him by threatening his guard?"

"I wanted to see how willing the upper class would be to sacrifice one of their minions. What it meant to them. I needed to test him to get a better understanding of their resolve, their feelings, and to get an idea if the rest of our plan had a chance to work.

"And did you get the information you wanted?"

"I believe I did, and with a little luck, I think we have a better chance now of getting away."

CHAPTER 36

While John readied the ship and inspected everything, making sure the Devorex didn't sabotage anything, Brian laid out the plan to the others. It was simple and elegant, however, he still asked for suggestions, ideas, concerns, or alternative courses of action. No one came up with anything better.

"We'll have maybe one shot at this," Brian stated. "If it goes to hell in a handbasket, there's a good chance we won't survive. If we do, we must quickly get back to the planet and somehow get Jack to the spires to get rejuvenated. Only then can we focus on exposing the High Scribe and his wicked plan."

"That's not going to be easy," Frank said. "We won't be able to get the ship anywhere close and they will be looking for us. What do you intend to do?"

"First things first," Brian said. "Let's get out of one predicament at a time and then we can work on the next one."

After making sure they were under their influence by the effects of the mind control devices, instructions were given to all the Devorex involved in the plan. The two remaining emissary guards were put off the ship with their own instructions.

John and Frank were at the controls of the Hiimori while Brian and Paul strapped themselves into chairs. Jack was placed on a table and strapped down. They could be in for a rough ride and Brian didn't want to worry about him in his weakened condition. Blue Robe and their new small alien friend were in the other section of the ship.

There was nothing left to do except wait for the prearranged signal with one of the zapped technicians who controlled the locks holding the Hiimori, the bay doors to open space, and their possible freedom, or an impending doom.

Suddenly, a loud horn sounded that could even be heard inside the Hiimori. The intervals between the blasts became shorter and when they became one long, annoying sound, the bay doors opened, exposing the blackness of space. Large robotic arms connected to the main ship moved to the Hiimori and took hold of the ship. The locks securing the ship were released and the arms moved it into a position just outside the bay doors. The Hiimori being held just outside the bay doors was released with a push from the big arms and she drifted away from the Devorex's massive ship.

Frank adjusted the controls and the Hiimori began to slowly move away under its own power. Again, Brian could see the enormous size of the Devorex's ship as they got further away. It still took up the whole viewing area. To say it was occupied by thousands of the small Devorex creatures was sure to be a gross understatement.

"Hold on," Frank gave a warning, "I'm initiating the

main drive and getting us out of here before they get wise."

"I missed the meeting," John began. "Why aren't they shooting at us? Not that I'm complaining."

"Why would they?" Brian said. "We're not escaping, we're on an important mission sanctioned by one of their diplomats who happens to be on board our ship. As far as they know and from what they have been told by his guards, he has been invited to the planet to negotiate a timeline with the High Scribe himself to get all the humans he has in stasis transported to their ship just as he promised them. They will remain in this sector until he returns. They think the dinner bell is being rung."

"But what happens when he doesn't return and there are no humans transported to the ship?" John asked. "I don't think they will respond to that very well. They may act against The People and our world. These are not patient nor reasonable creatures. They are small minded and very aggressive in nature."

"You don't have to tell me. They might seem civilized to some degree, but I've seen and felt their primordial nature and their animalistic desires. No matter how cordial they may seem, they are very dangerous and not to be trusted. We'll deal with the Devorex ship and the rest of the little scaly lizards as soon as we get Jack rejuvenated and the High Scribe exposed and in custody."

"What are you going to do with Blue Robe and the little soldier who is helping us?"

"We'll deal with them after we get the High Scribe," Brian stated. He didn't care what happened to Blue Robe, but he felt a sense of appreciation and a touch of loyalty to the soldier, Yet, he was still one of them. He would have to think about what course of action he needed to take, but not now.

The ship was now headed back to the planet and Brian needed to come up with another plan to get Jack to the rejuvenating spires in the middle of the city without getting caught. There was not one of The People on the planet to turn to for help.

The little ragtag group of misfits was on its own against a powerful and corrupt High Scribe who held the Guardian of The People, the Council of The People, and an entire planet at his beck and call. This was not going to be easy.

"We're going to need some help," Brian stated.

"And where do you expect to get that?" John asked.

"Where do you turn when you are at the end of your rope or you find yourself with your back to the wall? You get help from some heroes," Brian replied with a smile.

CHAPTER 37

"Put the ship down there, for now," Brian said to Frank, pointing out the ship's front window to a place along the cliffs. "it should be safe."

Brian went to Jack who was now seated in a chair. "I may need your help with this, my friend, if you feel up to it."

"I will try," Jack said, "but I believe in you and your ability. Don't forget, it's not just your mind, it's your heart. You are a good person, just as was Sarangerel. They will know."

Brian helped Jack to the ship's transportation disk and together, they left the ship and positioned themselves over one of the falls of the honey-colored liquid. The flying horses, the Hiimori, were frolicking in the air and running majestically atop the cliffs. Each time Brian witnessed them, he was in awe of their ability, their beauty, and just how magnificent they were.

Brian had the craft land and he and Jack walked to an open spot where several of the horses grouped. A couple flew off, retreating to the caves among the cliffs, but several, including one who looked a little older than the others, were cautious, but unafraid of their presence.

"Don't try to communicate as you would with me," Jack advised, "open your mind and let them feel you."

"They can do that?" Brian asked, amazed. "How will I know?"

"It may be strange for you, the first time, but all creatures have a way to communicate. You may not comprehend it, but you will feel it. It may not be a language or even an exchange of ideas, but with some patience, and the willingness between two beings, a type of understanding might come to light. That's how Sarangerel was able to befriend them. I believe you can too."

"Do you really think we can do this? We need their help right away."

"Only if they allow it. Sarangerel is the only person, even of my own, who I have ever seen permitted to fly with them. It was a great honor for her."

Brain walked out ahead a few steps, held his hands out to his sides and closed his eyes. Trying not to think too much about what he wished, he thought of how beautiful the horses were, how they were strong and noble, how they were companions to brave men, warriors for righteousness, heroes through the ages.

Brian opened his eyes, expecting to get a reaction from the flying horses, but they had not moved and even seemed to be less interested. He turned and looked at Jack, giving a gesture as to ask, "Now what?"

"They know who they are," Jack stated, "let them know who you are. Be open with them, allow them to feel your desires, your dreams, even your faults, and vulnerabilities."

Brian turned once more to the multi-colored horses. He took a deep breath and slowly exhaled. Closing his eyes once more, his mind traveled to thoughts of home, Earth, and the beauty he'd seen, all the people now gone, the sadness he felt, the crushing loss of his wife and the hunger for the sound of her voice just once more, the softness of her touch, and the little smile she would give when she told him he was loved. He missed her, and that sadness weighed heaviest on his heart.

A tear escaped the corner of his eye and slowly traveled down his cheek. He started to raise his hand to wipe his face, but he stopped as he felt a heavy, warm breath on his face. He slowly opened one eye and saw that one of the wind horses had come up and was face to face with him. It was the eldest looking of them and it appeared as if the horse also had a tear running down from one of its eyes as well.

The wind horse was larger than most of the others and they all were larger than Earth horses. Its massive wings were folded back along its flank. It nodded his head up and down as to invite an interaction.

Brian slowly raised his hand and caressed the dark horse's powerful neck. Immediately he felt a strange connection with the creature. Not a telepathic reading of its mind, but something deeper.

He felt the edges of a deep sadness within the horse but there was also the remembrance of a time, a time long ago when this wind horse was young and full of spirit, when it flew through the air, happy and unafraid of the human female who spoke with a soft voice and showed a gentle heart. She was trusting, kind, and would laugh as they flew together most days in those times. She was a special being.

One day, she didn't come to the cliffs. He waited for her, but she failed to come again the next day and then the next. He didn't stop waiting for a very long time. Flying was not as fun anymore. He missed her laugh.

The wind horse moved away from Brian and began walking over towards Jack who he knew as the female's friend but stopped short. He flared his nostrils several times and then blew out a mighty breath, not liking the sickening odor of decay he was smelling before turning and flying off.

CHAPTER 38

On the way back to the ship, Brian relayed to Jack what he felt within the wind horse, how he kept guarded what happened to Sarangerel, not wanting to upset the empathetic creature.

"Maybe we should," Jack stated. "Doesn't he have a right to know the truth as well?"

"Would that really make things any better for him?" Brian asked.

"What if they wouldn't tell you about your wife for weeks after you woke up after the accident? Would not knowing make you feel better?"

"Of course not," Brian said with a tone of anger. "I had to know. There's no way they would have kept that from me. It's not the same."

"Maybe not to us," Jack said, "but to him? It's just like my needing to know what happened to Sarangerel. I knew somehow the High Scribe was involved but I didn't have any proof. Over many of your years, I formed a plan, made the necessary arrangements, and finally found the one human I believed could help me bring justice to Sarangerel.

"Is it justice or revenge you seek?" Brian asked

"Maybe both," Jack relayed.

Jack was looking worse. The wind horse could smell his body deteriorating. He was no long iridescent, he was now a pale-grayish, sickly color. More times than not, he was wobbly, unsteady, and needed to support himself while he stood. He needed the rejuvenation process to happen soon.

They arrived back at the ship and Brian got Jack back into a chair. It was best to keep him stationary and let him rest.

"I know what you want to do," Jack said. "It's a bold plan. I have something that might help."

"You need to stay right here until we can make sure we get you into the city without getting caught or worse," Brian stated. "It won't be long, I promise," he said, praying he wasn't just giving false hope.

"There's a device in one of the bins," Jack said, raising a shaky arm and pointing one of his ten fingers towards the command console area. "I want you to take it with you next time. I want you to tell him, you need to tell him—" Jack's thoughts became jumbled and almost too weak to read. His head slumped, and his body went limp.

"We need to put him in a stasis pod, now," Frank said, "or he won't survive much longer."

They gently picked Jack up and carried him into another part of the ship where he was placed into a stasis pod not unlike the one Brian had been in after leaving Earth.

"Even this will only delay what will happen unless we get him to the city," Frank said. "Whatever you are going to do, you need to do it now," he said to Brain.

Brian went to the control console and opened the bin Jack indicated. Inside was a small circular device. It appeared to have several controls on it.

"I know that piece," Frank stated. "I made it for—for Jack just after Sarangerel died."

"Show me," Brain asked, handing it to Frank.

Frank operated several of the controls and set the device on the deck of the ship.

A life-sized image of Sarangerel appeared, similar to what Brian witnessed in her quarters when she was murdered, only this time, she was happy, smiling, laughing. She was talking to Jack, reaching out with her hands. It was so real, Brian wanted to reach out and touch her, and he could have if he allowed himself, but this was not for him. It was Jack's memory, and it was being placed in his custody.

An idea came to Brian. "Frank, could you make me one similar to this if I gave you the proper information?"

"It's possible, there is a recording device here on the ship, but I would have to do most of the work in my lab where all my equipment is located."

"How long?"

"It's pretty simple, maybe a few hours."

"Can we take Jack's pod off the ship?" Brian asked.

"The pod is self-contained with its own power supply," Frank said. "It could last years at normal use, unfortunately, Jack doesn't have that much time."

"How long can Jack survive in stasis?"

"In his condition, no more than a couple of days at best I would think. After that, it won't matter. The process will be irreversible."

"That settles it. I'll give you the details for the new device, then you and Paul will head back to your lab to complete the job. The rest of us will stay here, getting things ready for when you return. We'll take the small disk and Jack's pod along with our Devorex guest. They shouldn't be a problem. If I think Blue Robe starts getting other ideas, I'll zap him again. We'll hide out in one of the large caves along the cliffs.

Brian gave Frank the details he wanted for the new hologram device and they spent a while together away from the ship. When they returned, Frank and Paul prepared the spaceship as Brian and John put Jack's pod and the Devorex pair on the small disk, maneuvering it to a spot on the plateau overlooking the honey-river valley.

The Hiimori lifted and headed away from the planet leaving the small group. Brian now had some work of his own to do.

CHAPTER 39

Brian still needed to get the wind horses to agree to help with his plan. Without them, his hopes of getting Jack safely back to be rejuvenated might be dashed. Jack trusted him, and Brian did not want to let him down to die an agonizing death.

Brian knew what he must do and hated to do it but to get the Hiimori to assist, he needed to get the elder horse to not just join them, but to get others to help as well. That may not be easy to do, but Jack gave him a bit of leverage.

Brian left John and the others, walking along the cliffs until he came to the spot where he first encountered the big, dark horse. It was not there, and he did not see it in the air. He sat and waited. He watched others fly around the falls and over the river. Several times he would see one go into a cave or come out of one to spread its wings and fly to join the others.

Brian continued to wait. He tried to reach his mind out and make a connection with the horse, to any of them, but to no avail. After a long while, he got up and was about to leave when he saw the big wind horse emerge from the mouth of a high cave.

It leaped into the air and spread its large majestic wings, beating them just a few times to gain altitude. It glided in a circle high above Brian before finally settling down just a few feet from him. It stood looking at him and then slowly moved the few steps it took to be within reach.

Instead of reaching up to the horse, Brian pulled Jack's hologram device from his pocket and placed it on a large flat rock and activated the controls.

The image of Sarangerel materialized, her voice carried to him softly and clear. The wind horse backed a few steps, obviously surprised. his nostrils flared several times and there was a look in his eyes that could only be described as joy.

"She's not really here," Brian tried to relay, but the horse either could not understand or didn't want anything to do with Brian right at that moment. The female human was back.

The wind horse took several steps, pushing his head into the image of Sarangerel's outstretched hands. The horse moved his head around but was unable to make the solid contact with the kind and sensitive human he had known so many years ago.

The horse took several steps back, shook his head and again moved forward in an attempt to touch the human female, but again without success. A different look now settled in the horse's eyes.

Brian reached down and turned off the device and the image disappeared. The horse seemed to stare for a few seconds in wonder and then let out a severe whinny as he reared up on his hind legs, kicking his front legs high in the air, and coming down with a loud clap that echoed like thunder throughout the valley.

The wind horse did not understand what was happening. The female human, his friend and flying companion whom he had not seen in eight hundred years was there one moment and gone the next. He heard her voice. Her laugh. The soft, strange sounds she made and yet, he couldn't smell or touch her.

The horse was delighted to see her, excited and yet, confused at her sudden appearance and then just as quick, her disappearance. What did this other human have to do with her? This strange human man who he was compelled to examine through their brief bond and who held such a deep longing and sadness within his own being. But there was more. There was a connection between his female friend and the man. Not one of desire or belonging. Not one of friendship or even a kinship. It was something new and different for the horse. It was something the human called justice and with it, a darkness that shrouded it he called revenge.

Why would this man need this justice and revenge for his friend? He needed to explore this more. Find out where she had gone and if she would be back. What this justice and revenge were and why the man wanted it. And not just for this female.

The wind horse approached Brian as he had done the first time, offering himself to be touched to allow the more solid and personal connection between the two. This would only be the second creature other than his own kind the horse had ever made a connection with.

After a very long while, the wind horse slowly backed away. He turned and headed back to the cave from where he had emerged, the mighty wings seemed to slump, and his powerful neck and head hung low. Brian could swear he heard the wind horse moan as he slowly walked away.

Brian returned to the group waiting for him atop the cliff. He was drained from the long, emotional connection with the wind horse. John placed a hand on his shoulder.

At first, it did not understand the technology of the hologram depicting Sarangerel's image. It took some time of repeated explanations to get through. It took even longer for the horse to accept what had been Sarangerel's fate at the hands of the High Scribe.

'Accept' would not be the right phrase, but the wind horse finally understood why she never returned, although he could not fathom such intentional cruelty. He also seemed to understand the meanings of justice and revenge and what Brian was trying to achieve for the female human who was called Sarangerel.

Brian knew the mighty horse was in pain with the revelation of the tragic loss of his friend, even if she was a human and by ordinary human standards, it was so very long ago, but he needed to get his help for his plan to work and to save Jack. However, the horse wanted nothing more than solitude right then and he would not be denied.

CHAPTER 40

When "Jack" made the request in front of the Council, the High Scribe voted against a human police detective being brought back from Earth for the purpose of investigating the death of another human.

She was only a human being, not one of The People, and it could have been an accident anyway. The police detective would be another inferior being for them to take care of, to be wary of, and to be contaminated by. It was a waste of time and resources he preached to the Council.

In one of the rare occasions since becoming the High Scribe, he was overruled. The others on the Council believed it would be a grand social experiment, however, they cautioned "Jack" he would be responsible for the human and once the experiment was over, the police detective would be placed into stasis or disposed of in a prescribed manner.

"Jack" agreed. He never advised the Council of his feelings about how Sarangerel met her death, believing it not to be an accident or who he believed could be responsible.

He presented the Council with the idea of observing humans who used their intelligence and expertise to solve complex problems involving other humans and he believed a human police detective would fit that qualification nicely. He added that one day, they may be trained to communicate with The People in their own language and ways.

The situation with the human female known as Sarangerel presented them with a very unique situation because there had not been a death of a human on their planet, other than natural causes, except for Sarangerel's "accident" over eight hundred years ago. It had almost been forgotten, but not by "Jack".

The Council was willing to go along with "Jack's" request because several on the Council were curious as well as concerned about the humans and their development. Many of the humans who were brought to the planet for various reasons were evaluated and some were specially trained. Some were found to have abilities allowing them communication to operate the flying disc and even some, with The People. Sarangerel was one.

The Council wanted to find out more about their development, the reports about their ventures into space, and how soon they might travel into deep space. The rest of the Council believed it to be a good idea to keep them under watch.

The High Scribe believed humans to be dangerous to The People and their world. He thought of humans as a disease. He formed his own secret network to get rid of the humans; on his world and theirs.

He held these feelings even before he was deformed by

the human female. But she was different from other humans brought to their world. She had abilities far advanced of others. He wanted her for himself; to teach, to research, and to experiment on, among other nefarious things. However, she showed a strong attachment to the one who found her on Earth and brought her to this new world.

The High Scribe knew she must have used her abilities to poison his mind, make him weak, causing him to lose his way. She may even have been able to turn him against his own people and ideals. She and the rest of her kind were evil.

The High Scribe believed he was superior among all The People and even the Council. He knew what was best for their world. He would not just be the voice of reason, but the only one who could save them from themselves.

The Cleansing had been used by The Ancient People to rid The People of the problems of emotional thought and action. Selective breeding, education, training, and control turned them into a society of apathetic beings, logical and focused, but he felt because of his superior intellect, he had been spared the effects of The Cleansing, allowing him to retain and use the forbidden emotions, aggression, and thoughts as a tool to eventually rule The People and to become their savior.

The High Scribe is a dangerous psychopath, a self-serving megalomaniac, and more than that, he is totally insane.

William N. Gilmore

PART FIVE

William N. Gilmore

CHAPTER 41

Brian maneuvered the small disk along the far cliff face between two of the falls as some of the wind horses flew high overhead, keeping their distance from the strange, wingless craft.

He was looking for one of the caves, hopefully one that would be unoccupied, where they could hide until Frank and Paul returned from the lab. He hoped it wouldn't be long.

The two Devorex, the little soldier who deserted and Blue Robe, did not like the flying disk. They both sat holding tightly onto the secured stasis pod Jack was in. They seemed especially frightened by the aerial creatures, clicking back and forth excitedly while keeping an eye on them.

Brian was able to catch some of their rapid conversation as they talked about how big and powerful the creatures were. Blue Robe even wondered how they would taste. Brian had to stop himself from throwing him over the edge of the disk and into the honey-colored river far below.

Brian noticed the magnificent, ancient wind horse come to the mouth of his cave. It leaped high into the air, spreading his massive wings and with little-perceived effort, flew up to the now stationary disk. As it glided closely past Brian, he looked him in the eyes and gave a loud whinny and swishing its tail.

The two Devorex cowered, holding onto each other as they tried to hide their heads and giving out little squeals of terror. Blue Robe quickly lost his craving for a taste of the creature, hoping he would not be its meal. John laughed.

Brian believed the wind horse wanted him to follow and had the disk land just inside the mouth of the cavern where the large winged horse waited, but he was not alone.

There was another wind horse further back in the cave lying on a thick bed of dried grass. This wind horse was a brilliant white, not as big as the stallion, but she was obviously very pregnant.

Brian left the platform of the disk, walked along the rocky floor of the cave and up to the stallion. Placing his hands on the horse once more, he learned the mare was not just his companion, but the dominate mare of the herd of wind horses. She was soon to give birth to their first foal, but there were some complications as there many times were with the birth of a winged horse. The chances for survival was very low for both the foal and the mother. His companion was in distress and in danger of losing the yet unborn foal. They needed help.

Brian had little experience with horses, much less with birthing one. His wife, Angie, was the country girl, living on a working farm most of her life and helping with all the chores and animals that come along with it.

They were on a visit to her family farm not long after

getting married when they were requested to help with a cow having problems giving birth. The calf was large and if they couldn't get it out in time, it might die of oxygen deprivation.

Brian watched in fascination. He saw Angie do things he could never do. She reached inside the cow to check on the position of the calf, making sure it was turned correctly, although she couldn't tell if it were still alive. No matter, it had to come out to save the cow and there was only one way to do that.

Cows usually give birth while standing whereas horses give birth while they are laying on their sides. The calf would usually come out hind feet first and a foal would come out front hooves first; if you were lucky.

Most births, even ordinary ones were complicated enough, but with a wind horse, because of the structure of the wings, it put so much more strain on the foal and the mother. A breech birth would have dire consequences for both. He hoped this would not be the case.

The dark stallion was asking Brian to help his companion as this was her first foal. This birth was special in another way as well. This would also be the first foal born in several hundred years and would help to continue the lineage of their kind.

Brian wished Jack was well enough to be able to help, maybe give some advice or support. He was on his own except for John who had no experience at all and you could forget the Devorex. But he couldn't just stand there and do nothing.

Brian told the stallion to go and get more of the long, dried grass, a lot of it. Not that he really needed it, it got the father horse out of the way and he didn't want him to see what he was going to have to do.

He had John undo the bindings holding Jack's pod to the disk as he went over to the mare and attempted to soothe her. She was breathing rapidly and noisily. She attempted to raise her head, but Brian laid his hands on her, making the intimate connection.

The mare reacted to the joining by giving a loud moan and blowing air out her nostrils but otherwise did not attempt to rise. She had also known and connected with the human female.

Brian wasn't real sure what to relay to the mare, he didn't want to show his awkwardness or nervousness, so he started out introducing himself and how he came about being there. He made sure she was as comfortable as much as was possible for the moment and told her what he was about to do. He couldn't believe it either.

Brian first went to the tail of the mare, wrapping it so it would not get in the way. The mare's water broke just a short time ago when she laid down on the grass bed.

As he saw Angie do with the cow, Brian inserted his hand into the horse's birth canal. A quick inspection indicated the foal was coming out head first as it should, and its hooves were very close to being visible.

The mare was straining and pushing, becoming more vocal with small squeals and moans. The edge of a translucent white sack started to appear containing the foal for birthing. A single hoof began to make its way out and shortly after, another. An almost rubbery protective coating covered the hooves. The front legs were out to around the knees, but the nose and head were not free yet. The size of the foal was creating a block.

The mare continued to push and strain, but the foal had stopped its exodus. After several very tense minutes without movement, it was obvious the foal was in serious trouble and therefore, the mare was in trouble as well.

Brian went into quick action, knowing what he must do even if it wasn't exactly something he had been trained for. The birthing sack was already broken allowing him to grab the hooves of the foal, wrapping his shirt around them because they were slippery and to protect the legs of the unborn horse.

At first, he started to pull gently, putting more muscle into it as the resistance continued. The foal did not budge. There just wasn't enough force to get the large foal out.

He took some of the binding and wrapped it around the hooves and got John to help. Together, they pulled on the rope trying to get the foal out, but again, they were not enough.

Time was getting short. If they didn't get the foal out very soon, it wouldn't be delivered alive. The future of the wind horses themselves may be in jeopardy if they failed.

Brian looked over at the Devorex. Even with what little help they might be, it wouldn't be enough, and the Stallion had not returned, either.

Brian looked at the Devorex again. Well, not at them so much as at the disk. He hurried to it and got on it, maneuvering it close to the mare. He tied one end of the rope around the shirt-covered hooves of the foal and the other to the disk. He had John get back on the disk and slowly take up any slack of the rope and went back to the foal.

As Brian held onto the legs of the foal, he had John very slowly move the disk away. It was painfully slow, but it was working. The foal's nose slowly appeared and then the rest of the head. The most difficult parts would be the shoulders and wings, then the hips.

The mare gave out some agonizing groans and squeals, but the foal was being delivered, one way or another.

Just as Brian thought the foal was stuck again, the mare gave a mighty push and the foal came completely out of the birth canal and onto the bed of grass.

As the just delivered horse lay in the dried grass, the umbilical cord still attached to its mother, Brian could see it wasn't breathing on its own. The mare raised her head and strained her neck to look. She let out a mournful cry that echoed throughout the cave.

Brian, tears in his eyes and biting his lip, suddenly

remembered other things Angie had done when a calf was being born. He stuck his fingers into the little horse's nostrils, cleaning them out, and then grabbed handfuls of dried grass and began rubbing vigorously on the small creature's sides and chest.

He did this for a few minutes, calling out loud to the newborn to breathe and wake up, for it to open its eyes and see the wondrous world that would be his.

As he continued to rub, there was movement. The young colt, with a little difficulty at first, inhaled. Coughing and sneezing, clearing its passages, as it began to breathe the lifegiving air, he opened his big eyes and started moving his head. The legs began to flex, and even the nubby wings seemed to stretch.

Brian, with a wide grin on his face, removed the rope and his shirt, tossing them back onto the disk, almost hitting the two lizard-like creatures in their astonished faces.

He gave John a thumbs up and then he helped move the weak, new colt to lie at the side of his mother. She immediately began bonding with her new colt by cleaning him.

Brian turned and saw the big stallion standing behind him with a mouthful of dried grass. The dark wind horse was gazing with pride at his new son lying beside his mother. He was a beautiful, dark colt, just like his dad. The mighty stallion's mouth opened in awe, dropping the grass. What may have been seen as a tear was in one of his wide-opened and proud eyes.

Brian had one too.

After a short rest, the mare slowly stood. This allowed the umbilical cord to naturally break and gave her better access to her newborn to clean him. The colt himself would be up on all fours in about an hour and would be able to nurse for the first time. It would be much longer before his wings fully developed and he would be able to take his first flight.

The new father was out spreading the word of the healthy birth of his son and the good condition of the clan's matriarch.

When the wind horse returned to the cave, he went up to Brian and nudged him. He was thankful for what he had done, saving his companion and his son and maybe their future. The wind horse's numbers had been dwindling.

Brian connected with the horse and was given some instructions. The horse moved to some rocks where Brian scaled them to be able to mount the tall animal. He straddled its back just behind where the wings formed out of the horse's shoulders. He began leaning forward a bit, for balance and afraid he might hit some of the low hanging rocks on the roof of the cave.

He held tightly onto the long, thick mane, wrapping his hands deep as he had been told to do, afraid of what was about to come. He sensed the horse's thoughts of him being heavy, cumbersome, and awkward, not like the small, human female.

The wind horse began to gallop to the entrance of the cave which was just a few feet away. Brian could feel the strong muscles of the horse, the wind as they gained speed, and then suddenly, the horse bounded from the cave and into the open, pinkish sky.

Brian slammed his eyes shut, his legs clamped tight against the horse's sides, and his fists clenched in fear of falling. He was also afraid he would throw up, but his excitement quickly overcame his queasiness, even to the point that he lifted his head some and ventured a quick peek with one eye.

He was flying. It wasn't like the Hiimori or even the disk. He felt this. The flapping of the horse's wings, the openness with the wind in his face, and the fear of actually falling off.

He gripped a little harder to the mane if that were even possible. He had no control and was at the mercy of the horse, yet he knew he could trust him, not fear, and gave in to just enjoying the ride.

The wind horse flew up and around, merging with some of the others while they were in flight, giving a series of vocals, ear twitches, tail swishes, and head nods they seemed to understand. Some of them flew away and joined in another formation, dropping to a place on the plateau and landed.

As they settled, about a dozen of the other horses formed a semi-circle. Some appeared almost as old as the dark stallion, but it was hard to tell. The wind horses lowered their heads, showing respect to the lead stallion.

Brian slipped over one side of the horse and dropped to

the ground. The dark wind horse then made a point of going to each of the other horses, spending just a few moments with each one. A couple seemed agitated and blew air out of their noses, shaking their heads as they did, but there were no other signs of hostility. They knew their place and were not willing to challenge the stallion. More times than not, a horse would nod its head, sometimes adamantly.

Soon after the dark horse met with the last horse of the group, they all took off for the skies above the falls, leaving Brian and the stallion on the plateau. The big wind horse walked over to Brian, offering the connection once again.

Almost all of this wind horse council, at least, the eldest of them, knew the human female and were stunned to learn of her fate. The wind horses valued their solitude in the valley, not comfortable with having too much contact with The People or any other creature.

Sarangerel was different.

Her thoughts were pure and sincere, simple, and yet, very expressive. One of The People who sometimes accompanied her was unusually kind and caring, not like others. She trusted him and there was a strong bond between them. He was accepted as her mentor and companion.

The wind horse council having received the information from the lead stallion about the human female's fate, the human male's involvement, how he saved the mare and her colt, and the High Scribe's evil plans, agreed to assist Brian with whatever they could in saving his friend, and in seeking out this so-called justice for their ill-fated, human female friend.

Through the big stallion, the wind horses came to know the human female and her companion from The People. For harm to come to them at the hands of another, by one of The People no less, was unimaginable.

Now, they know the human male called Brian, who saved the clan's mare and her colt, who is a protector and an enforcer of laws on his Earth, who was brought to their world to make others accountable for their misdeeds, and is desperately trying to save a friend, and possibly, both of their worlds.

William N. Gilmore

CHAPTER 42

Brian was alone with the flying disk down by the bank of the honey-colored river trying to wash his shirt out. He left the rest of the crew at the cave with Jack's pod and John watching the little Devorex to make sure they behaved.

As he wrung out the shirt, he heard a noise high above him. He looked up and saw all the wind horses vacating the space above. The shrill he heard got louder until he finally saw what was causing it. Something was coming through the sky, leaving a smoky trail behind. Brian at first thought it was a meteor, but then it turned several times. Meteors don't turn.

It was the Hiimori and she was in trouble. Not far behind it, another ship was now visible, trying to catch it and firing its weapons at the Hiimori.

As the Hiimori maneuvered to avoid the weapons discharge, it was rapidly approaching the ground and would have to pull up soon. Whoever was controlling the Hiimori, if it was being controlled at all, was a skilled daredevil, a desperate fool, or insane; and quite possibly, all three.

The Hiimori continued its descent towards the ground, returning fire on the other ship that was much larger, faster, and easily outgunned her. It was gaining quickly as well. If the

267

Hiimori didn't pull up now, it never would.

Brian watched but he was too far below ground level and the ships were still several miles away for him to see clearly.

The ships were soon out of his sight, however, just a few seconds later, he heard the far-off explosion and soon felt the ground tremble as one or both ships crashed, or one was destroyed by the other. The chances for the Hiimori were not good.

Brian rushed to the disk, hopped on, and put it into motion towards the crash location. As he got some height, he could see a column of smoke several miles away. There were no ships in the air.

He thought of Frank and Paul and how their deaths might affect Jack once he was rejuvenated, but now with their loss, it seemed less likely he would get the opportunity. He was now rushing to the scene faster than he had ever gone on a disk but wasn't sure if there would even be anything he could do once he got there, or if there would be any remains to recover.

As he got to the site of the crash, everything was burning; ship debris, trees, bushes, even dirt. There was a crater, fifty feet deep and several hundred feet wide. Neither ship was distinguishable. There certainly wasn't anything to recover.

He landed the disk a short distance away and walked through some of the smoldering ground just to see if there was anything that would tell him about either ship.

As he peered over the edge of the crater to its bottom, a figure came up beside him on his left and began looking down as well. Another joined him on his right, and said, "What a mess."

Brian first turned to the left and saw Paul, then turning to his right, he saw Frank.

"How…?" Brian's eyes went wide as he looked back and forth at the two and tried to speak. "Why…why aren't you—?"

"Dead?" Frank finished for him.

"Yeah, that. And who was in the other ship?"

"Supporters of The High Scribe," Frank said. "Or, at least they were. He has several ships loyal to him set up as blockades around the planet. When we tried to return from the moon where my secret lab is located, they tried to stop and board us. We weren't going to have any of that. As soon as they were close enough, Paul opened the valves on the storage tanks holding the waste from the human sanitation facilities on board onto their main viewing port. It gave us just enough of a diversion to get away and give us a head start for the planet."

"So, in some fashion," Paul said, "you contributed in helping us get out of a nasty jam. Thanks."

"Happy to have been of service," Brian laughed. "But still, how did you manage to not be splattered at the bottom of that crater? The way I understand physics, that would have been impossible."

"You keep referring to Earth science," Frank stated.

"This isn't Earth, or haven't you noticed that yet?"

"So, how did you get the ship out of that steep dive in time?"

"I used a little bigger device than the one I made for Jack. It projected a long distance hologram of the whole ship. While I was working on the device you commissioned, I had a crew working on the Hiimori. She was already equipped with a stealth shield to make her seem invisible, I just added a little more. So, the ship they were chasing wasn't us, it was a ship that wasn't even there. The Hiimori is parked just over that ridge," Frank stated.

"She did receive some slight damage though," Paul said. "The damage was to the hyperdrive, life support, and a few other minor things. She'll fly, but she won't be doing any faster than light travel for a while and until we fix the life support, I don't think it would be a good idea to submerge her."

"She's been good to us," Brain said, "let's take good care of her. How long will the repairs take?"

"Just a couple of days, I would think, if we can get the parts. Just a little longer if we can't." Paul surmised.

Brian gave Paul a funny look and just shook his head.

"So, anything exciting happen here while we were gone?" Frank asked.

CHAPTER 43

Brian kept a constant watch on Jack, checking his condition and that the pod was working correctly. He was getting nervous they wouldn't get to the spires in time. Jack wouldn't survive long outside the pod once they opened it again. They needed to make sure they were free from interference and had an uninterrupted time for Jack to do what he needed to do.

Brian was still unsure what the process was and how long Jack would have to have contact with the spires. It wasn't like jumping off a dead battery. He was sure Jack, in his weakened condition, would need to have a prolonged session with the spires. It only made since.

Frank and Paul were working on the Hiimori. There was nothing Brian could do to help. He wasn't that good under the hood of his own car, so a faster than light drive was a little out of his expertise.

He had the device Frank made for him and was testing it out in the cave. He thought it worked pretty well and hoped it would be useful.

He sometimes ventured a look over at the mare and her new colt. If the newborn colt wasn't sleeping, it was nursing. He wouldn't take more than a few steps away from her.

The mother regained most of her strength and would let the stallion watch the colt as it slept while she would go out and graze, but she wouldn't be gone too long. If the young wind horse woke while she was gone, even with his father there, it became scared and let out some piercing squeals that echoed throughout the cave and would reach the mare who hurried back, much to the relief of the stallion.

Over the next couple of days, several ships passed slowly over the area, surely at the direction of The High Scribe. Some gathered around the crash site, apparently looking for the Hiimori, and specifically for Jack and Brian. They were too well hidden within the caves and using the stealth abilities still working on the Hiimori, but they wouldn't be able to hide forever. Jack's time was almost up.

Things were a little different for Brian being the one on the run and hunted as a criminal. Of course, being hunted on an alien world was a little different too.

Brian was sitting on a rock in the cave fine tuning his device and waiting for word from Frank on the status of the Hiimori when the dark stallion came up to him, nodding his big head indicating he wanted to connect with him. Brian stood and put his hands on the wind horse.

The connection lasted some time and Brian was wide eyed and had a slight smile on his face when he finally put his hands down. The stallion surprised him with information that was a well-kept secret, known only to the wind horses. It was information that might be the turning point in getting Jack to the spires without the High Scribe stopping them.

The stallion had to get permission to share the information from his mare, the leader of the clan, and the wind horse council. It was something that had been a secret part of their culture since the first wind horse flew the skies over this land. It's why they made their home here, lived and died here, and never left.

William N. Gilmore

CHAPTER 44

The High Scribe was getting perturbed. The idiot human and the conspirator he calls "Jack", because he is too stupid to use the language of The People, could not be found. Reports of "Jack's" ship returning from one of the moons and being intercepted by a lookout seemed to be verified. "Jack's" ship refused to stop and be boarded, and a battle ensued. Both ships headed for the planet with at least one of them crashing. There were no survivors from the horrific, high speed crash and all evidence was destroyed right along with the ship and crew.

The traitor's ship was obviously back on the planet, but where? He had ships searching, informants out trying to find an unguarded thought, humans who were bribed to give word if they were spotted, anything he could to stop them. He knew "Jack" would need to get to the spires soon. He had entrances to the city guarded. Time, something that had never been anything to worry about, was now the enemy of both sides.

Too many resources were being used to be able to keep the hunt quiet for much longer. The Council would want to know more information and he would have to be untruthful again. All the lies were adding up and hard to keep straight in his ancient mind and hide from deep probes if the Council decided to investigate further.

He must get rid of the human and all the ones he contaminated and poisoned against his authority. He was the High Scribe after all. His will was the law. Well, it very well could be, very soon.

The High Scribe called for a meeting of the Council and once all were in attendance, demanded he be named The Supreme Ruler, a position that was abandoned when the Council was formed after the time of the Cleansing.

The position was deemed too powerful to be held by just one of The People without the checks and balances of an oversite committee. It was finally agreed to have a Guardian of the People who would be the head of a Council with additional members holding high office such as Vice Guardian, The High Scribe, and The Gun Maker. Lesser positions, yet with an equal vote would constitute the remainder of the Council.

All in all, there were supposed to be seven members of the Council, but with the location of the recently reinstated Gun Maker unknown, only five others were present. As The High Scribe addressed them with his demands from the front podium, there was much protest and grumbling amongst the others.

The High Scribe had some reluctant support from one or two, but the majority refused to even consider the High Scribe's demand and were calling for him to resign and to present himself for re-education. In other words, for him to go through the

Cleansing again.

This wasn't going to happen. The High Scribe knew the Council needed to have a unanimous vote to take such drastic action. With The Gun Make not present and his whereabouts unknown to the rest of the Council, they were unable to force him into the re-education. Even so, he knew the members who showed him support in the past would not cross the rest of them on this issue. The High Scribe had gone too far and made demands that were not in the best interest of The People.

He knew the Council was about to act against him. He knew it was coming and he was prepared, but he wanted to give them a chance. They were his People.

The High Scribe turned his little disk and without another word, left the podium and the Council room. The members of the Council continued to discuss the arrogance of The High Scribe, his bold demand, and the fate he should face. Suddenly, there was the sound of loud clicking coming from the outer halls.

The extreme silence in the Council chambers and between the remaining members was extraordinary. It only made the clicking outside the chamber that much louder. As the clicking seemed to be getting closer and even louder, the Council members huddled together around The Guardian of the People.

The persistent clicking reached a deafening climax as there was a sudden flood of a green, scaly tide into the chamber. Nothing could stop the small lizard-like Devorex as they took part in a feeding frenzy of the defiant Council members.

The High Scribe, through his dealings with the Devorex superiors, obtained the use of a squad of hungry Devorex soldiers, secretly bringing the small collection of Devorex to the planet, keeping them sequestered and barely fed until he needed them.

He would use them as his personal enforcers for when he knew the Council would surely rebel against him, setting them loose upon the ingrate defectors.

With the rest of the Council member's elimination, he was now the ranking member. He nominated himself for the position of Supreme Ruler, voted on it, and passed it into law. There were no objections noted.

Now, he needed to find the Gun Maker, "Jack", and the inferior human and serve them up to the Devorex as well.

The High Scribe, or now in his new position, The Supreme Ruler, was quickly becoming the planet's first serial killer.

CHAPTER 45

Brian was on the big stallion again, flying over the river and through the mist of one of the honey-colored falls when it suddenly dove into the falls itself. The torrent of the water-like liquid nearly knocked him off before the wind horse landed at the entrance of a cavern concealed by the falls.

Brian ran his hand over his hair and face like a squeegee before he jumped down from the horse, allowing it to shake the water off himself. Regaining the connection with a hand on the stallion's neck, Brian stated a little perturbed, "You could have warned me. I almost fell to my death in the river."

There was no response to Brian's comment from the wind horse, except for a snort of air and water from its nostrils.

"So, what is this?" Brian inquired. "Another home for one of your group?"

The wind horse advised this was the entrance to a secret passage and relayed he wanted Brian to follow him on foot. The roof of the cave would sometimes dip too low for him to ride and in the darkness, he could injure himself. The footing could also be dangerous, and the stallion suggested Brian hold on to his tail.

Unknown to Brian until now, the wind horses possessed the ability to see in total darkness. This allowed them to fly in all weather and even on the darkest nights. Brian held tight to the long tail just as he did to the horse's mane while they were flying.

The stallion took him on a path that twisted through the rock on the inside of the cliffs. The path had a gradual decline at times and became a little steeper in other places.

The pace was slow as they continued on the zigzagging path. Brian, unable to see anything, even the horse right in front of him, resisted the urge to put a hand out. There were times when there were puddles he waded through and smooth rocks that were slippery. Several times he bumped into a boulder with an arm or shoulder or hit his knee on an outcropping rock, almost letting go of the horse's tail.

Strange enough, Brian was able to maintain the connection with the wind horse through its tail. The wind horse made sure he was not going too fast for the two-legged human and checked to see if he needed to rest.

After about a half hour of Earth time on the rocky trail, Brian hit a rock jutting out from a formation with his shoulder. The surprise hit almost turned him completely around. He was forced to let go of the horse's tail, losing the connection as well as his bearing.

Brian reached out in the dark with both hands, feeling around and taking very small steps while attempted to feel something, anything, hopefully, the wind horse. He called out to the horse, but only got back an echo.

As he moved slowly in one direction, something swatted him in his face. It was the horse's tail and he took a big step just as he grabbed for it. When he did, one foot met with empty air and his momentum started to carry him completely off the solid ground. He began to fall and with one hand, grabbed in desperation for the horse's tail.

Brian was dangling over a ledge, one hand tightly gripped around the stallion's long tail and the other flaying out in the dark before he was able to reach up and take a two-handed grip on the tail.

The sudden stop and Brian's weight caused the wind horse to begin sliding backward on the slight plane of slick rocks towards the edge. Brian knew they were in serious trouble, especially not knowing how far of a drop was below him, and with the wind horse losing the battle of getting any traction and continuing to lose ground towards the ledge, it wouldn't take much to send them both into the void.

Brian would not allow himself to be responsible for the death of this magnificent creature, a new friend, and a new father as well. He resolved to accept whatever might happen and was about to let go of the horse's tail when the winged stallion took a powerful leap, flapping the mighty wings with all it had, carrying Brian up and over the ledge to safety. In doing so though, the stallion struck the ceiling and several rock columns hard, falling to the dark floor of the cavern with Brian still clutching its tail. Neither moved for a very long time.

CHAPTER 46

The Devorex was a very old species. No one knew just how old. Savage, barbaric, and militaristic, they somehow were able to acquire the intelligence for advanced thinking and space travel and then spread throughout parts of their own small sector of the universe, conquering worlds, acquiring their technology, depleting their resources while using the inhabitants as their main source of food.

The Devorex society was made up of different factions including a warrior class, a diplomatic class, a science class, a working class, and a servant class.

Early in their development, the warrior class was the dominant and ruling class, but over many years and many conflicts, the diplomatic class rose to a prominence of their own and slowly was able to use their superior intellect over the violent predispositions and short-sidedness of the military structure.

However, overpopulation and the need for ever increasing food resources forced them to expand their search outside of their known part of the universe.

Invading several peaceful planets and enslaving the populations allowed the Devorex to expand even further into space. In doing so, they came across a ship of creatures who were their superiors in both intelligence and power. Creatures who referred to themselves as The People who possessed the ability to speak in thoughts.

The People knew the intentions of the Devorex and when information reached the Council, the spread of the Devorex before it became more of a problem for The People would have to be dealt with.

Although they were not experienced at war, The People were well advanced and armed to deal with one if the need arose. However, they were more inclined to be diplomatic and sent emissaries to meet with the Devorex, that included The High Scribe.

Treaties were made with understandings about encounters and boundaries in space. The Devorex agreed they would not enter their system without advanced notifications, there would be no exchange of technical information, and there would be no invasion of other worlds.

The High Scribe, unknown to the Council, made his own secret deals with the Devorex, offering a ready supply of food for the time being and even providing the promise of future information of a world with an almost endless supply for the Devorex. A place called Earth.

Now that the Council was no longer a problem, he put out a planet-wide restriction on all ships leaving; except those under his authority. He ordered most of the ships to search for the traitors. He suspected the old Gun Maker had a secret base on one of the moons. The ship bringing them back from the secret base seemed to have survived somehow. The ship that encountered them on the return was unable to give a trajectory before it crashed and so the High Scribe still did not know which moon to search and there would be too much area for the few ships he could spare.

He sent a few of the Devorex back to their mother ship to advise their leaders to help conduct a search of the moons for the hidden base. As an added incentive, if they found it, they may take possession of all the occupants and then destroy it.

As a further goodwill gesture, he sent along several dozen stasis pods with humans in them as a gift.

CHAPTER 47

Brian was sore. He received a few cuts and bruises, but he was alive. He no longer had hold of the wind horse's tail. He made his way up to his head placing his hands quickly on the horse. It was laying on his side, one wing flayed out, but the horse was also alive, breathing heavily with a raspy sound.

"Please be okay," Brian pleaded more to the heavens than to the horse.

"I will heal," the horse responded to Brian. "But, let's not do that again."

Brian couldn't help but to laugh. Getting on his feet slowly and back to being serious, Brian inquired, "Are you injured badly?"

The wing that was outstretched began to move and folded back and forth a few times. Each time, the horse grunted. He got his feet under him and stood on all fours, moving them around. The other wing did not appear damaged.

"It may take a few days, but I will be alright.

"Thank you," Brian stated, "for saving me."

"You are my friend. I did not want to lose you."

"I still can't see very well, and you are hurting, should we turn back?" Brian asked.

"There will be light soon. I am well enough to continue. We must do this to save your friend."

"Light? Down here?" Brian asked, confused.

"You will see. Take my tail again. Be careful."

"I will."

They traveled the path for several more minutes. It was obvious from the sound the stallion was limping slightly on one of its hooves. Brian was about to ask if it was much further, hating for the horse to be in pain.

Just ahead, Brian could tell it was getting a little lighter. He could see the outline of the big horse in front of him.

The cave path emptied into a much larger cavern. The ceiling must have been several hundred feet high with the other end out of sight. There was a soft, rose-colored hue emanating from somewhere in the cavern giving light to every corner, not unlike what he first saw in the room he was in on Jack's ship during the journey from Earth. He was able to drop the horse's tail now with enough light to see.

The path was now wide enough for them to walk side by side. Brian was able to see firsthand the injuries the gallant wind horse had received. There were several open wounds and the left front leg was raw below the knee and still bleeding from a deep cut.

As they continued through the cavern, Brian heard a faint roar echoing throughout the cavern but couldn't discern the direction from where it was coming. They came to a long bend in the path. Once they were on the other side and in the open, Brian stopped in his tracks, his mouth agape.

In front of him was a large pool of the honey-colored liquid. It was really like a small lake. However, it wasn't the pool Brian couldn't believe that took his breath away, across the pond was a statue of a wind horse, carved out of the rock of the cavern. The statue must have been a hundred feet tall and fifty feet long. The horse was rearing up on its hind two hooves and appeared to be beating the rock wall with its front hooves. There was a wide stream of the golden liquid falling to the pond from where the horse statue appeared to be pounding the wall.

The wings of the wind horse carving were outstretched and were sure to be at least two hundred feet across. But again, that's not what Brian was awed about. Sitting upon the horse was a helmeted figure with a shield and a very long spear. The figure was human.

"What is this?" Brian asked, his hand shaking against the wind horse's neck.

"This is the creation of the Hippocrene; the horse fountain, and part of our beginning" the big stallion stated proudly. "This is Pegasus, the first of us. He is the son of Poseidon and Medusa. The human is the great warrior Bellerophon, who killed the hideous monster, Chimera, with Pegasus' help."

"But this is an Earth story. I studied Greek mythology in school. These are characters from poems and songs of ancient Greece. They're not—they can't be—real, not here." Brian stammered, still not believing what he was seeing. They continued their trek forward "How old can this be?"

"It is as old as it is. It is before my time and before my father's father's time. The human, Bellerophon, did not come from your Earth."

"What are you saying? He was from another world?"

"There was a time when there were creatures that were like humans, yet not, and then there were humans introduced to your world. The humans flourished, and the others became extinct."

"So, what you are saying is humans came from some other world and did not originate on Earth? Did they come from here?"

"No. There are many worlds where humans have lived and still live. Just as there are many worlds where my species live. The universe is vast."

"Who came to this world first?" Brian asked, stunned at the revelation.

"This is a world of many creatures. It is not important who came first. What is important is who will survive and continue to take care of this world."

"There are so many questions in my head," Brian began,

"I don't know if I can keep them straight."

"I will try to answer what I can, but there are others who may be able to answer better. What would you like to know?"

Looking at the big statue, Brian started with: "Who carved this and what does it mean?" Brian inquired, still not able to take his eyes off the magnificent sculpture.

"It is unknown or forgotten. It was told that Pegasus was able to extract the liquid from the rock by pounding it with his hooves, but this is more than just a pool of liquid. It is a living force arising here from the very core giving life to everything on this world. The spires in the city are only a small part of its power If you bring your friend here, you can heal him."

They had gotten to the edge of the pool and the big stallion waded into the liquid. Brian watched as he got up to his neck and then went out of sight under the surface. He'd never seen a horse on its own accord go completely under water before.

After just a few seconds, the wind horse resurfaced and slowly walked to the shore, snorting, blowing out his nostrils. There seemed to be a marked change in his appearance. He was no longer limping, and the leg wound seemed to have disappeared. The wings were strong and sound. Brian couldn't believe the quick change in the horse's condition.

Once out of the liquid, the wind horse moved up behind Brian and nudged him in the back towards the pool.

"Now, wait a minute," Brian protested out loud. "I'm not

a pegasi, nor am I of this world. I don't think this will work for me."

The wind horse continued to push Brian to the edge of the pool and just as Brian attempted to turn and protest once more, the horse gave a strong push sending Brian plunging towards the liquid, face first with his arms and legs sprawling in empty air. He gave a yell and hit the liquid creating a large splash that almost overshadowed the sound of the falls.

He broke the surface gasping for air and trying to get his feet under him. His head dipped below the surface several times before he was able to finally get stable. He swam a bit and then was able to walk out of the pool, dropping at its edge.

"What the hell was that for?" Brian gasped, trying to catch his breath again.

The wind horse gave a snort and a whinny as he nodded his head several times. Obviously, a horse laugh.

Brian then noticed one of the cuts he had on his arm begin to heal right before his eyes as if it were a time lapse film. In just a few seconds, there was no evidence there had ever been any damage to his skin. He checked a deep cut he had on his leg and couldn't find it. It apparently was also healed. Brian was stunned. He realized he felt good, really good.

"This is a secret we have kept to ourselves for millennia," the wind horse advised. "You are the first outsider permitted to take part in the healing of the waters of the Hippocrene. We believe that without you and the help of your friends, we may lose our home."

"The High Scribe is unaware of this place?"

"Not one of The People has ever been to this place."

"My friends and I will do all we can to stop the High Scribe of The People, to protect your families, your homes, and your world, and to seek the justice Sarangerel deserves."

Brian just realized he was not in contact with the wind horse, yet there was no problem in communicating with him.

"It is one of the benefits of the healing waters. It not only heals the body but the mind as well."

"I've been drinking the water of this planet since I've been here, but it hasn't affected me like this. Why now?"

"This pool is fed directly from the spires that come from deep inside the planet. The natural potency is not with any other source, even in the city."

"Then we must hurry and get Jack down here. I'm glad we don't have to take him to the city after all. However, I need to confront the High Scribe and the only way I can do that is to go there.

"It's not good to meet a foe on their own territory. They have the advantage. There are too many things to go wrong."

"Yes, but I hope to have a little help from an old friend who just may give me an edge. At least, that's what I'm counting on."

"You are also a great warrior, Brian, just like Bellerophon, but this time the monster that needs to be vanquished is the High Scribe of The People."

"Well, let's hope for the same outcome," Brian said.

They began the long uphill journey back to the initial cave entrance. Brian had some things on his mind.

"May I ask a few questions, just so I can understand some things better?" Brian asked.

"Of course, you may ask what you wish," the wind horse stated.

"First of all, do you have a name the others call you or Sarangerel called you?"

"I have a name that you as a human cannot say."

"Oh, that again," Brian stated, remembering the strange, unpronounceable sound that was Jack's name. "Did Sarangerel have a name for you?

"Not as a name like you have. I learned that in her culture, they do not give individual names to their horses. In her native language, she called us all Hiimori."

"Yes. That relates to her translated phrase, wind horse. So, the first of you, Pegasus, who named him?"

"The gods."

CHAPTER 48

Frank and Paul were nearing completion with the repairs to the Hiimori. It took a little longer than expected because of all the ships in the area looking for them. Even though they were in a cave, they had to make sure they did not alert anyone to their presence by making too much noise or allow the broadcast of energy waves from the ship, so every time a ship came near, they shut everything down.

They wouldn't be able to test all the systems before taking flight. They needed to do some patching that was more than a little uncertain, and they were skeptical everything would hold together, however, once in the air, it would be too late to turn back, unless of course, in the worst case, they fell back.

They added to the hull's integrity to withstand any strong weapon hits from other ships and increased power to their own weapon's system as well, adding a few surprises, courtesy of the two Gun Makers. The engines needed a little tweak too.

While Brian was away, John took the two Devorex to assist Frank and Paul with anything they could on the repairs. He still wasn't too sure about Blue Robe, so he kept a close eye on him and kept all his body parts away from his snout.

The little soldier continued to show he was not a

problem and helped watch Blue Robe with his many eyes. Frank just wanted to shoot the Devorex emissary, probably both of them and be done with it. He held no love for the Devorex.

Frank, before he was given the name by Brian, and the title of Gun Maker by the Council, was another who missed the Cleansing. Not by design, but by circumstance. He was out in the universe playing scientist, exploring, looking for things that might be useful for his many experiments. He was considered young, ambitious, and sometimes even rogue at times.

He traveled through many systems, sometimes finding an unknown inhabited planet, or one that was abandoned for unknown reasons, sometimes meeting strange, new beings, and sometimes, having to run for his life.

Frank became so focused on his goals; obsessed with finding just the right gizmo, the best chemical, or the perfect mineral, many times getting so close to what he needed just to be denied, he forgot he would need to rejuvenate within a cycle. The trip home would take almost that much time. If he didn't leave right then, he might die before getting to see his world one more time, but he couldn't leave yet.

He was meeting with a new group tomorrow. A group of reptilian beings called the Devorex. They possessed a mineral he heard about and searched for during this recent adventure. He was excited but knew to be cautious. Their reputation for dealing with strangers and not being satisfied was vicious. Many traders and explores were seemingly never heard from again after one meeting with the Devorex.

There were many rumors and stories about them. One report in particular was unsettling. They were strange, little, carnivorous beings, not too fussy about where they got their meat, but feasted on it while it was still alive. Worlds they conquered were nothing more than warehouses for food.

They didn't use energy weapons except on their ships, preferring to use a type of personal capture weapon to keep the subject alive and unharmed for future use.

Frank wanted to trade advanced technology for the minerals. Hoping the Devorex were advanced enough to understand its importance but also its danger.

He knew there would be a language barrier to begin with although his ability to pick up their language through their thoughts would make it easier. He didn't know they communicated in audible clicks. When he was able to see their thoughts, it was crude, unfocused, and terrifying. How they ever were able to advance to obtain space travel, was a mystery.

The Devorex's thoughts were consumed mainly with sex, food, and…well, that was about it for the lower ranks, and the higher ranks were just a little more development in their little, green heads. They had planning, strategy, and development.

For Frank, the meeting went well. He was able to walk away not only with several kilos of the rare mineral he needed, he didn't even suffer any nips or bites from the hungry teeth of the little lizards.

The technology Frank gave them in exchange was dangerous and he warned them repeatedly of the risks. If only they had paid attention and listened. Many lost their lives when the Devorex either refused or failed to properly utilize it. It was even possible they tried to alter the properties, enhance the productiveness, or increase the output of the device.

The Devorex were lucky they had not brought it to their home world and only to one of their minor moons. Many ships observing from afar were still too close. Many of the hierarchy of the Devorex; military leaders, diplomats, scientist, and many more were lost. Their regime structure was torn to pieces, just as their moon had been.

Even with his willingness to meet in person, to make fair trades, his insistent warnings, the Devorex blamed Frank. Orders were put out to capture him. His future, as short as they wanted it to be, was not going to be pleasant.

When Frank was found to be part of a crew on one of The People's ships that was seized, there was much discussion about what to do with him and the rest. The People's High Scribe with whom they had a pact, was contacted. He also wanted Frank and especially the human.

Now, with all of them escaping with one of their diplomats as hostage, the Devorex had a new and bold plan.

CHAPTER 49

Brian and the stallion, both healed from their injuries and exhaustion, made their way back to the cave entrance hidden by the falls. With the knowledge of the healing powers of the horse spring in the cavern, Brian no longer needed to take Jack through the city and somehow past the High Scribe to get to the spires.

The healing waters of the golden pool within the deep cavern were more effective than the spires rising up in the city and the High Scribe had no knowledge of them. They just needed to get Jack there in time.

Brian got back to the group as they worked on the Hiimori and told them what had occurred. He showed them his healed injuries. There was nothing to see. As they prepared to get the pod in which Jack was confined ready for transport, a group of Devorex scout ships arrived and began searching the area.

All the other wind horses who were flying in the area fled to their own caves or other areas away from the danger. More ships arrived. A few were even of similar design to the Hiimori.

One of those ships slowly approached the entrance to the cave where the Hiimori was located. It stopped and hovered there for a few moments. Brian half suspected it would open fire on them.

After a short while, a rear hatch opened, and a small craft exited. It was the High Scribe on his small disk.

He entered the big cave alone, slowly approaching the group now taking cover towards the rear of the cave behind the Hiimori. Brian put his hand on the grip of his 9mm pistol that was in a holster strapped on his waist under his shirt.

"No need to fear me at this time," he sent out. "I am here to demand your surrender. You are trapped and there are a dozen ships, both of the Devorex and The People in the area ready to destroy all of you if you try to harm me or try to escape."

"And what if we do not surrender?" Frank inquired.

"You will all be destroyed here in this cave."

"What happens if we do surrender?" Paul asked quickly.

"This is not a negotiation," the High Scribe declared. "You will either surrender or not. I hope you say you will not."

"What does the Council have to say about this?" Frank asked.

"The Council? I am the Council. I am The Supreme Ruler of The People," he said, citing the old, pre-Cleansing position of absolute authority. "There is no other voice."

"What did you do to them?" Frank demanded to know.

"They sacrificed themselves for the good of The People."

"In other words, you murdered them," Frank lashed out.

Brian had to hold onto Frank to keep him from going after the High Scribe. He knew he would not come into the cave unarmed and believed he had some type of weapon hidden under the cloth covering his missing appendages. One of his hands was in that area and hadn't moved since coming into the cave.

"Will you give us time to talk about this?" Brian asked.

"You must return the Devorex diplomat and soldiers to their people," the High Scribe stated. Brian could sense the disgust for him in his thoughts. He could also feel treachery. Trust was never a consideration. "This may give you a few minutes, but time is short. It is difficult to hold them back from tearing the flesh from your body and the meat from your bones."

"The Devorex diplomat and the soldier may return if they wish, however, I do not believe that is the case," Brian said.

"Then you have brainwashed them. I would suggest you prepare for what is to come. I have seen it firsthand."

"Leave us," Brian said. "You will know our answer shortly. We will send out the Devorex if they wish to go."

The High Scribe backed his disk out of the cave, not turning until he was well outside and returned to the ship from which he came.

"Now what do we do?" An anxious and visibly shaken Paul asked. "If we don't surrender, we all die, possibly horrible deaths. I'd rather not be eaten alive."

"I don't see anything different if we do surrender," Brian said. "He's mad. I don't see us getting out of this without a fight."

"We have one ship, they have at least a dozen," John finally made a comment. "The odds are not looking good."

Brian shook his head. "If we surrender, Jack dies for sure; maybe all of us. If we can't get Jack to the pool in time, he dies. If we fight, we won't last long, and we will probably all die, but it will be on our terms. I know what I would do, but I can't answer for the rest of you. Let's take a vote."

"Take a vote on how we're going to die? I don't think so," Frank said. "I say we…"

Frank was interrupted by a series of loud clicks. They came from Blue Robe. He was very agitated and insisted on being heard. He wanted to know why he and the soldier were not consulted on the matter.

"I'm not sure he can be trusted," Frank said. "They still want me for what happened to their moon and the High Scribe has made them some serious promises."

It was the little soldier who started clicking in earnest this time. He and his superior had been collaborating while everything was happening, and they came to a decision.

"So, our little friend wants to abandon us now that things have changed," Frank said. "Fine. Give them back to the Devorex or shoot them. I don't care which. I'm tired of them."

"Let's hear what he has to say before we make any rash decisions," Brian insisted.

The little, green soldier went on a clicking concert.

CHAPTER 50

The High Scribe was made aware Brian and his band wanted to have a face to face meeting to discuss the Devorex hostages. Brian insisted there would be no tricks and the High Scribe could bring as many of his own guards or Devorex soldiers as he wanted.

In short order, the High Scribe arrived alone on his disk to the entrance to the cave. His arrogance and smugness shone through to Brian like a beacon. He was daring for them to do something. He moved further into the cave.

"The Devorex diplomat and the only soldier we have wish to be turned over to you," Brian stated.

"What happened to the other soldiers?" The High Scribe inquired.

"There was an unfortunate accident and they are no longer with us."

The tiny soldier clicked to the High Scribe, confirming Brian's story. The High Scribe saw within the strange, simple brains of both little creatures that this was the truth.

"The Devorex may not take this information well," the High Scribe said with hope they would want to seek revenge on Brian and his group. The type of revenge that would leave their bones picked clean.

"This is one of the reasons we are releasing these two," Brian stated. "We hope there can be an understanding."

"I'm sure they will understand," the High Scribe sent the cryptic response. He sent for a transportation disk to come and take the two Devorex back to one of their ships. When it left with them, the High Scribe again started to retreat.

"We will contact you soon with our decision about the surrender," Brian said.

"You have ten minutes," he told them, "then we will open fire and kill everything in this valley."

"Wait, there's no need to do that," Brian insisted, not understanding the High Scribe's reasoning "Why would you do that to all those innocent horses? They are creatures of your own world. You have nothing to fear from them."

"I would destroy them because you have infected them, just as Sarangerel did. You have contaminated them with your human touch just as you and all of your revolting kind have done with everything you have made contact with on my world. It is time to rid my world of your human infestation and influence. Your ten minutes start now." He turned and headed back to his ship.

"Let's move," Brian said, "we don't have much time."

"You really think they will be able to pull it off or are they going to change sides again?" Frank asked.

Not sure if he was asking because he still didn't trust them or that the task would be almost impossible, Brian just shook his head, stating "It's all we have, so as they say on my world, we're damned if we do and damned if we don't."

"Does that mean we lose no matter what we do?" Paul asked nervously.

"No, Paul," Brian tried to console him. "It just means that no matter what we do, it's going to be difficult to overcome the obstacles in our path but giving up is not the answer either."

"Neither is dying," Paul said. "And it sounds like the High Scribe is going to make that very easy for us."

"Let's finish getting Jack secured on the disk," Brian said. "then we can get ready for everything else we need to do."

"What about the wind horses?" Frank asked. "Shouldn't they be warned about what's to come?"

"They have been," Brian confirmed. "I've been in contact with the stallion. They know their part."

Brian and John made sure Jack's pod was secured on the disk. It might be a rough ride, or a short one.

Frank and Paul were making the final adjustments to the Hiimori.

The ten minutes were almost up when they all boarded the ship. They gave each other a look and a nod. Frank took his seat at the command and Brian took his position with Jack. Paul and John strapped in. It was time.

CHAPTER 51

The High Scribe was on his ship with a full view of his armada made up of The People's and Devorex ships. A strange smile showed on his little slit of a mouth. He was relishing in the anticipation of what was about to come next.

He was about to give the order to fire upon the cave where the Hiimori was located and where his human antagonist along with the other traitors were cowardly hiding.

He hoped the attack would not kill them, just break down their resolve and have them surrender so he could prolong their suffering. Maybe, one at a time while the others watched, he would let the Devorex have their turn with them. What a delightful thought that was.

Their time was up.

Just as he was giving the command to fire, his own ship rocked as it came under fire from somewhere above them. A lone Devorex ship suddenly broke from the formation and began an attack run on the High Scribe's command ship, disrupting the plan to fire on the cave. It had to move from being a stationary target and receiving more damage.

As it moved away, the Devorex ship fired on several of the other ships, making lucky shots that destroyed one of the

High Scribes collaborators and severely damaging one of the other Devorex scout ships, putting it out of commission. They had not thought they would need their protective shields.

The rest of the combined fleet was caught off guard again as they saw the Hiimori fly out of the cave and up into the sky, apparently heading for space. It got a good lead, making it just out of range of their weapons, but many turned and quickly pursued it. The rest went after the rogue Devorex ship.

The High Scribe's ship did not follow. It was damaged, listing badly, but somehow maintained its ability to fly. The High Scribe was incensed but otherwise unharmed. He demanded the Hiimori be captured and the rogue Devorex ship destroyed.

With only the High Scribe's damaged ship remaining in the air, the Hiimori, the real Hiimori, exited the cave. Frank had rigged a rocket probe with a hologram device like he used earlier to give the impression the Hiimori was flying out of the cave. It was hoped the distraction would give them time to escape from the cave. It worked.

The Hiimori didn't head for safety, instead, it headed for the falls that hid the other cave entrance. It wasn't far, but they still had to deal with the High Scribe's ship.

The entrance to the cave behind the falls was not large enough for the Hiimori. It would get close, but Brian would have to go from there alone, exposing himself to the High Scribe's ship and weapons. It was a risk, but one that had to be made.

The High Scribe's ship dove on the Hiimori, firing its energy weapons at almost point-blank range. If not for the extra protection Frank and Paul had fabricated, the Hiimori would not have lasted long.

As the Hiimori got close to the falls, dozens of wind horses flew down from the cliffs, setting up a blockade and a screen.

Brian flew out of the belly of the Hiimori on the transportation disk with Jack's stasis pod secured to it. Once clear of the ship, he headed straight for the falls.

The High Scribe wasn't about to let a few flying horses get in his way. He opened fire on them as he powered on towards Brian, but for some reason, the energy weapons had no effect. He wasn't far behind Brian and he thought he could ram through the horses and might get lucky and hit him. He gave the order to accelerate the damaged ship right through the horses and straight at Brian.

Brian just about made it to the falls when he turned and saw the High Scribe's ship mowing a path through the wind horses, knocking some of them out of the air, with broken wings and bodies falling to the river below.

The ship was almost upon him as he entered the falls. He pushed the disk as fast as it would go, just making it to the entrance of the cave as the ship was coming through the falls.

The ship, a little smaller than the Hiimori was still going

quite fast as it started to enter the cave, its sides gouging into the rock as the integrity of the hull gave way. The low ceiling of the cave ripped open the top of the ship as it turned sideways and slid along the rocky, damp floor. It came to an abrupt stop by a solid rock wall that crushed the front of the ship.

Brian maneuvered to the back of the cave near the path to the larger cavern. The disk barely had room to make it through. He waited to see if there was any movement from the ship and not seeing any, he started towards the path.

The High Scribe was tossed from his small flying disk onto the deck of the ship. The pilot and the rest of the crew were dead. A large upper section of the ship was jaggedly torn back like a sardine can. Power was offline. All the systems were dead. It would never get out of the cave the way it came in.

The High Scribe was dazed. He crawled his way to his disk. It took a bit, but he finally got it working. He found Sarangerel's gun he had kept hidden under the cloths that also hid his missing legs. He also decided to take one of his dead security officers side arms. It might come in handy as well.

When he finally made it out of the ship and into the open cave, he was confused as to Brian's intentions. *"Where are you going, human? Why are you in this maze of rock? Are you setting a trap for me?"* The High Scribe was querying only himself. *"For some reason, the human fled from one cave into this one. What is here? What is he up to? Let's go see."*

310

CHAPTER 52

Brian hoped the High Scribe had died with the spaceship crash in the cave, but he was afraid it wasn't so. He could still feel the evil thriving and it was very near to him.

He was having problems navigating the disk through the narrow walls of the path in the dark. He hit them several times, jarring the disk and the pod, afraid he would damage them. The pod was too heavy for him to carry and taking Jack out of the stasis pod was not a good idea. If he took him out, he would have to be very close to the pool. He didn't think Jack would now be able to survive more than a few minutes outside the pod.

If the High Scribe was following him as he believed, his little disk would make it through the tight pass and he would catch up quickly. Especially with him trying to carry Jack with care. It would slow him down considerably.

He thought about setting a trap or ambush for the High Scribe, but that would be too dangerous for Jack as well. If anything happened to him or the pod this far away. Jack would be dead. He had to push on and get as close as he could.

Brian's fears became a reality. He came to an impasse. The disk was too big to make it through the pass and would not be able to go any further. He could just see the beginning of the soft, rose-colored light coming from the cavern of the pool ahead. It would take about seven or eight minutes by foot to get all the way to the pool. He didn't have a choice on what to do.

Knowing the High Scribe was not far behind, he got the pod off and struggled to get it on the other side of the slim channel. He went back and wedged his disk between the narrow rocks, so the High Scribe would have a problem getting by. Anything to delay him, even for a few minutes.

He went back and activated the controls that opened the stasis pod. A hissing sound followed by a cold blast of air struck him in the face. He lifted the lid of the pod and picked Jack up, cradling him in his arms, surprised at how light he seemed, like a new puppy. For the moment that is. After a few minutes hurrying to the pool, he would seem to weigh as much as a Great Dane.

Jack's color was a dull gray, he had a discernable bad odor too; like death warmed over. Brian wasn't even sure he was still alive until he felt a very labored, single, shallow breath and heard the moaning exhale.

Brian knew the clock was ticking and he started to run towards the pool, clutching the small alien close to him to keep him from bouncing around. He wasn't sure how long he could keep it up. He hadn't run in ages. But this time, he was running not just for his life, but for someone else's as well.

CHAPTER 53

The High Scribe was in close pursuit of Brian and Jack. He couldn't have been more than a couple of minutes behind. He was attempting to maneuver his small disk along the tight path through the rock. Being in near total darkness didn't help.

He came upon the abandoned transportation disk Brian left. It was blocking the way with no room to go over it and would take some effort and time to remove it before he could continue. The High Scribe didn't have the time and wasn't going to make the physical effort.

He pulled the gun he took from the dead security officer out from under the cloth covering his missing limbs. This was a powerful blaster pistol. It would destroy anything, living or not.

He backed away what he thought would be a safe distance, adjusted the power on the gun to a minimum setting, aimed, and fired at the disk.

The disk exploded into a ball of blue and orange flame, rocking the High Scribe's small craft with the shock wave, nearly tossing him out. When he was able to recover, he saw the path was now clear except for small remnants of what had once been the larger transportation disk. He wondered what it would do to the human, giving another small, evil smile.

Brian stopped momentarily and turned, looking into the dark behind him in the direction of the sound of the explosion, knowing immediately what it meant. He knew the High Scribe somehow removed the obstruction and was not far from catching up with him.

Brian had one more thing he could do. He planned to use it to get in the city past the High Scribe, but now, he could use it as a distraction to buy him some more time.

At Brian's request, Frank made him his own hologram like the one he made for Jack of Sarangerel.

He made a recording of himself on Jack's ship and gave it to Frank when he went back to his lab. The recording was a loop lasting several minutes with Brian speaking to the viewer as if he were in front of them.

Using one hand, Brain took the device from his pocket and set it up on a rock for it to project his image on the path. It would activate when there was movement in front of it.

Brian turned and after taking several deep breaths, started running towards the healing pool once more. He had been right in that Jack now seemed to weigh a ton. His arms were getting tired from holding Jack close to him, not allowing him to run in a natural way with his arms pumping, drawing air. His legs were tightening, and he was afraid they might start to cramp.

Brian exited the narrow cave as it expanded into the large cavern with more light. That meant he was just a few minutes from the pool. That gave him a little extra strength in his legs and just a bit more speed. He was going to need it.

The High Scribe was hurrying as fast as he could down the path. He just came through a bend in the path when he saw Brian standing right in front of him, pistol in hand pointing in his direction. There was no way he could stop in time. He knew Brian would get a shot off and this close, he wouldn't miss, nor would he be able to get out of the way.

The High Scribe brought the front of the disk up to act as a shield as he held on to the sides. The tilted disk hit the ground, bounced, and skidded to a stop twenty feet past Brian.

The High Scribe was confused. He never heard a shot, nor did he feel the disk hit Brian. He looked back and saw Brian still standing in the same spot, pointing his gun down the path, away from him. How he missed him he didn't know. He brought his own gun up and fired. Brian should have been blown to pieces, but he still stood there. Now he realized it wasn't Brian at all.

William N. Gilmore

CHAPTER 54

After just another minute running that seemed to take forever, he saw the pool and the statue of Pegasus and Bellerophon. He was nearing exhaustion, gasping for air, but he couldn't slow down. Just behind him, a boulder exploded into thousands of pieces, some even hitting his back. The High Scribe was behind him about two hundred yards and fired a gun at him, just missing him.

Now, Brian began to run in a zig-zag to keep from making himself too good of a target. That slowed him down, put more stress on his legs, and allowed the High Scribe to get closer.

Brian wasn't more than twenty-five yards from the pool when the High Scribe fired again. The blaster's ray missed Brian and Jack, but just barely. It hit at the base of the statue of Pegasus, sending rocks and boulders flying in the air.

Brian had to stop and duck, covering Jack with his body from the flying debris giving time for the High Scribe to catch up even more.

"Do not try to run any more, human or I will destroy you and the traitor to The People," the High Scribe demanded, pointing the pistol at him from just a few yards away. "I doubt you are a hologram this time, or should I shoot and see?"

Brian knew if he moved, made any attempt to get to the pool, he would never make it.

"What is this place?" The High Scribe asked, not taking his eyes off Brian.

Brian, breathing heavily from the run, didn't answer. He wasn't sure he would be mentally strong enough now to stop the High Scribe's forced intrusion into his thoughts. He tried filling his thoughts with things, senseless things, to throw him off. It seemed to work for a bit.

"Put him down and step back," the High Scribe said, now hovering just a few feet from Brian's head.

"He's dying," Brian begged. "He needs our help."

"He's a traitor to The People."

"You're the traitor," Brian shot back. "You killed Sarangerel. I saw it all. And now, you've murdered the Council and you are trying to kill us."

"They didn't understand. You humans are a disease. You have your sick emotions, your needs, your greed, and you don't care about anything other than feeding your own desires. I didn't murder anyone. Everything I did was for The People."

While the High Scribe was ranting, Brian was slowly taking tiny steps backward, hoping he would not notice. He was right at the edge of the pool. He had to keep him occupied.

"You're trying to say that what you are doing is not your

fault because of your own preconceptions of humans? You're a monster. I've known monsters like you on Earth and I've hunted them down, brought them to justice, and made sure they never breathed free air again. You made deals with the Devorex and sent them humans to feast on. You lied about Earth being destroyed. You lied to The People for your own greed."

Brian felt the cool liquid of the pool at his heels. All he needed was just a few more seconds.

"I told you to stop."

Brian continued. "You knew what happened to Sarangerel, why did you let Jack bring me from Earth and why did you allow me to see what you did to her?"

"I knew he suspected I had something to do with her death. I couldn't stop the Council from allowing him to go to Earth, or it might have proven what he already knew. I did not believe your mind would be strong enough to make it as far as it has. You are truly remarkable, for a lowly human, that is."

Brian was up to his ankles in the pool. He was throwing everything he knew into blocking his thoughts while trying to keep the High Scribe at bay by talking. He had an idea.

"Why are you going into the water? You cannot escape," the High Scribe said, pointing the gun right at Brian's face.

Brian looked down at his friend. "Jack is dead. I couldn't get him to the spires in time." He looked back at the High Scribe with tears coming from his eyes. "There was a secret passage

319

that led to them from this cavern. I wouldn't have to go to the city and fight my way to them. Now, it doesn't matter anymore. I'm going to put him in the golden waters of his home and say goodbye one last time. Then, you may do with me as you will."

The High Scribe tried to confirm what Brian was telling him, but he couldn't get a clear reading. He was very skilled as a human. *Maybe,* he formed the thought, *he should kill him carefully and dissect him or maybe dissect him while he still lived.*

Brian slowly lowered Jack into the water. As light as he was now, he almost floated. He gave him a little push towards the middle. He walked slowly back to the shore, raising his hands, taking the High Scribe's attention away from the pool and towards him. He was expecting the High Scribe to shoot him at any time. He knew he wouldn't survive the shot from the blaster after seeing its power.

"Where is this secret passage you said goes to the spires?" The High Scribe demanded. "Show it to me."

Brian pointed up to the top of the falls where the statue of Pegasus' had his hooves striking the rock wall. "There."

"That does not seem likely," the High Scribe questioned, looking up. "I think you are lying to me."

When the High Scribe looked up at the top of the falls, Brian quickly pulled his 9mm pistol from the holster under his draped shirt and fired at him as he ran for cover behind a boulder. The bullet struck the flying disk, causing it to teeter for a second in the air. The High Scribe, surprised and knocked off balance, fired an errant shot from the blaster, hitting the rock wall by the statue, blowing rocks and boulders to the floor of the cavern and into the pool.

When the High Scribe was able to regain control of his disk, he flew for cover behind some rocks as Brian fired off several more shots, just missing him.

Brian knew he was outgunned. His projectile gun meant he had to hit what he was shooting at whereas the High Scribe only needed to shoot in a general direction to hit a target. He wasn't sure how many charges the blaster held, but he only had a few more bullets left. Once he was out, the game was over.

He moved around using the large rocks as cover and tried to get a look over at the pool to see if Jack was still there. In Jacks condition, he didn't know how long the healing might take if at all.

A loud explosion jolted him, and rocks were flying all around as the High Scribe, not knowing exactly where he was, took shots in his general direction. A large boulder he had been behind a few seconds ago was now a pile of rubble. At this rate, he would be exposed in no time.

He braved to look over the rock and took a shot just to try and get the High Scribe to keep his head down and not fire at him. He could wait for him to show his ugly head, but that meant he would have to show himself for a short time and that might be just enough time for the High Scribe to get a shot off at him. Also, it would give away his exact position.

Another boulder close to him exploded into thousands of tiny missiles, some with sharp points and edges cut him on his arms and legs. One hit his forehead and there was blood trickling down the bridge of his nose. He wiped it away as he moved behind another large rock.

He did a quick look and saw the edge of the hovering disk just peeking out from a rock. He took careful aim and waited, hoping to get a shot on its evil, little operator himself.

He was almost trying to will the disk out in the open to get the shot when there was another explosion of rock. This time, the blast wasn't directed at Brian, but was in the other direction; back along the path they came down to get to the pool.

Brian couldn't believe his eyes. Coming up the path, dodging between rocks and boulders, climbing over and around them, and scurrying as fast as his diminutive legs would allow, the little Devorex soldier was making his way towards the battle armed with only his tube weapon.

CHAPTER 55

The High Scribe was now being confronted on two sides as he tried to maneuver to get a good shot at the scaly alien. Brian couldn't allow the High Scribe to get a shot off and fired knowing there was no chance to hit him. His first shot ricocheted off a rock close to the High Scribe, drawing his attention back to Brian. His second shot never got off. The pistol was out of bullets, the slide locked to the rear, leaving Brian defenseless and now exposed.

The High Scribe turned his disk around and flew above the rocks he was concealed by. He had the perfect firing angle on Brian. As he got closer, he aimed the blaster and just as he was about to fire, the disk was jerked to a sudden halt.

The Devorex soldier had fired his own weapon at him, causing the tacky net it shot to strike and attach to the disk while the other end connected to the gun was now lodged between two rocks. The disk wobbled out of control breaking the sticky bonds, tossing the High Scribe down and to one side of its deck causing him to lose hold of the blaster pistol.

The disk started spinning and headed for the floor of the cavern. It hit the top of a boulder and careened towards the pond, skipping a few times on the surface before flipping and landing upside down, dumping the High Scribe into the golden water with him sinking below the surface.

Brian and the little Devorex ran to the edge of the pond, but there was no sign of the High Scribe.

As he stood there scanning the water, a familiar, inner voice asked, "What are you looking at?"

Brian turned and saw Jack sitting on a flat rock several yards behind them. He looked like his old self, even better.

"Jack!" Brian yelled out through his huge grin. He ran to his friend and lifted him up.

"And you thought I was dead," Jack teased. "You didn't have much confidence in me hanging on."

There was a rumbling sound and a large rock fell from the wall of the cavern, crashing to the floor.

"I knew there was still a spark left in you, you old coot," Brian said. "You didn't think I'd give up on you, now did you?"

"Never. I felt your commitment and dedication to our friendship. It kept me strong."

"You have a strength all your own inside you," Brian said, putting him down.

Another rock fell, splashing into the pond.

"How did you find this place?" Jack asked. "What is it?"

"The big stallion who befriended Sarangerel brought me here. This pool has the healing powers of the spires, but even more so. I think it's connected to the wind horses and Earth's past somehow."

The little Devorex soldier was looking up and started clicking rapidly. He covered his head with his small hands.

"He thinks we should head back before we get flattened by a rock," Brian stated. "Maybe we should."

"What happened to the High Scribe?" Jack asked.

"He went down with his disk. He probably died in the crash or he drowned," Brian said, nodding his head towards the pond. "Our little friend here saved my tail from being blasted into a thousand bits and pieces."

The little soldier could tell Brian was talking about him and gave a strange grin but kept looking up for falling rock.

"So, he's in the pond, now?" Jack questioned.

"It's been a while and he hasn't come up," Brian explained. "He's done for; finished. I can't sense him. It's all over," he said.

"Maybe," Jack said with uncertainty. "But there's something—not right; a presence that doesn't belong."

"You think he's alive?" Brian asked, disbelievingly.

As if on cue, the High Scribe broke the surface of the water. He made his way towards shore, walking with his lost appendages restored and pointing the recovered blaster at the astonished group.

CHAPTER 56

The High Scribe had the blaster tuned to the maximum setting. He wasn't sure what it would do to someone this close, but he was willing to find out.

"Before I blast you out of existence," he said with that smug little smile, "tell me how this is possible," indicating his revived legs.

"I don't know," Brian answered. "Somehow, the pool contains something more powerful here than the spires in the city. Where it comes from, I really don't know."

"Why is there a flying horse with a human on it carved out of the rock?" He asked, more awestruck than curious.

"There are things here that can't be answered," Jack intervened. "Maybe, they shouldn't."

Several wind horses suddenly appeared in the air above. First circling, then swooping down in formation like fighter planes about to strafe a target. The big, dark stallion was leading them. They had been watching the scene unfold below They possessed no natural weapons other than their hooves, but the wind horses, no stranger to acts of courage against overwhelming odds, refused to be watchers any longer. They knew what they must do.

"I think it's time to say farewell," the High Scribe began. "You have tried my patience too many times." He aimed right at Brian and fired. Or rather, attempted to fire. Nothing happened. He continued to try and get the blaster to operate, but for some reason, it would not discharge.

The little Devorex ran at the High Scribe and bit down on one of his newly regenerated legs. The vocal, primordial scream he let out was piercing as it echoed throughout the cavern.

Brian followed right behind the little soldier and wrestled the gun out of the High Scribe's ten-fingered grip as he tried desperately to get the jaws of the small but powerful Devorex off his leg.

The High Scribe went backward into the pool of water, dragging the soldier with him, striking the little creature on his head over and over until he finally let go and stumbled his way back onto the solid ground.

The wind horses made their way to the big statue and pushed against it, flapping with all their might. It started to creak and break, pieces of rock falling as it was forced from its already weakened mount by the shot of the High Scribe's blaster. It broke away with a loud crack from the damaged base and began to fall. As it toppled, it turned slightly with Pegasus and his rider, Bellerophon, headed for the pool.

The High Scribe saw the statue coming at him and tried to move, but the damage the Devorex did to his leg was severe and it had not restored from the healing waters yet. He moved back, deeper into the pool believing the falling rock horse would miss him and he was right, however, Bellerophon's long spear had set its sights on him.

He was knocked under the golden waters of the pool with the huge rock statue upon him, the ancient hero's extended spear impaled him and jammed deep into the rock bottom of the pool. He was trapped with no way to free himself.

The High Scribe in horrible agony, fought, squirmed, and held his breath until his lungs burned and finally gave up, forcing him to inhale the water, and slowly, painfully, drown.

He was soon revived by the healing waters of the pool and while being tortured with the searing pain of the spear still penetrating through his body, slowly drowned again, revived and then drowned again, and again, and...

The wind horses landed and the big stallion along with the others bowed their heads to Brian.

"Thank you, my friends," Brian said, returning the bow. "I am sorry your tribute is in ruins, but Pegasus himself would be proud of all of you today. You are all heroes."

"We are sorry it took us so long to get here," the stallion sent his thought to Brian. "We were dealing with the other ships. I'm happy to say they have all been rendered unfit to fly."

"And the rest of your group?" Brian asked, afraid to hear the report of horses battling against spaceships.

"We lost friends, some suffered injuries, but we have the Hippocrene to help with their recovery. The struggle is nothing compared to having our families safe and our world free again. Thank you."

Brian patted the wind horse on the side of his neck. He went to each one, laying a hand on them, showing his respect and gratitude, acknowledging their loss, thanking them for their sacrifice. Afterward, they flew off, heading back to their families. Their future looked a little brighter.

Brian turned his attention to his little, green friend. "And you," he began clicking. "Who do you think you are? John Wayne? You come charging in here like the cavalry, trying to get your little, green butt blasted off."

The poor Devorex was trying to click in.

"Not so fast, I'm not done here," Brian exclaimed. "You only had your little tube weapon against the High Scribe's blaster, and then you go and attack him not knowing if that gun was still working or not. Are you just plain one hundred percent bonkers?"

The little guy was still trying to get a few clicks in.

"Hold on," Brian insisted. "What was on your mind? Suicide? Do you have a death wish? Are you really trying to get yourself killed in the line of duty or something? Well, don't just stand there, what have you got to say for yourself?"

The Devorex hesitated before clicking anything to see if

Brian was done. Finally, he just had to know, "What is a John Wayne?"

Brian looked at the tiny soldier and couldn't help but laugh. "Just like you, he's a hero too." He grabbed up the scaly creature and gave him a big hug. "Thanks for saving my butt."

Brian put the creature down and patted him on the head. He turned to Jack. "What are you going to do about the High Scribe?"

"He has disgraced his position and his name, and it will be removed from the Halls of The People and from all places in the archives. Other than that,' he said looking over at the pool, "nothing—for now." He turned back to Brain and asked, "Is that justice, or revenge?"

"It's whatever you want it to be, but for now, it looks like a fresh start for The People. You're removing his name? Other than 'High Scribe', I didn't know he had a name. Well, I mean, I'm sure he had a name, of course, he had a name, I just didn't know it. I probably can't pronounce it anyway."

"He was first known by the name, Chimera. It is supposed to be a powerful, multifaceted creature. Something he envisioned himself and called upon it for its strength and diversity. When he was given the title of High Scribe, that is all anyone would call him, and his name was not spoken again."

"Are you kidding me?" Brian exclaimed, not believing the irony. "Chimera? That's the name of the mythical beast killed by the warrior Bellerophon, with the help of Pegasus. That's freaky. Two monsters of the same name killed by the same pair of heroes; one pair made of stone and the other, maybe or maybe not so much of a myth. History repeating itself on worlds so very different and so far apart."

When Brian and the rest returned to the cave entrance at the falls, they were met there by Frank, John, and Paul. They were all excited to see Jack and in awe at his renewed condition. They explained they were able to elude the other spaceships with the tricks and the added speed they infused into the Hiimori. Before long, the other ships for some reason gave up the search for them and returned towards the city.

Blue Robe saw his comrade and went running to greet him. He and the little soldier embraced. The clicking was so intense from them both, you couldn't tell who was more excited.

Everyone who hadn't been in the cavern or didn't know what the others had done to help, began asking questions. They wanted to know what happened to give the Hiimori its chance to escape, what happened in the cavern, where the High Scribe was, and all of them wanted to know what was next.

Brian wanted to know what was next as well. But mostly, he wanted to know if there was any chance he would ever see his Earth again?

PART SIX

William N. Gilmore

CHAPTER 57

They assembled in a group on the bank of the river where the damaged Hiimori was now sitting. Even the wind horses joined them. It was more than a celebration of their victory, it was an assurance of friendship, no matter their differences.

Whenever someone was telling their story, someone else would translate for those who either did not have the ability to read the thoughts, understand the clicking, or the alien tongue so they would not be left out.

The exaggerated and exciting stories were tossed around like hot potatoes. Praises and compliments, well deserved, were passed from one to another as well.

The little Devorex soldier clicked his accounts, with the proper translation by Frank of how Blue Robe used his position to commandeer the command ship of the Devorex fleet.

He used his position that is, after the little soldier talked Brian into letting him use the special pistol with mind control on his fellow beings. He came up with the plan hoping Brian would trust him with it and give him the instructions to use it on the other Devorex. It was much better than killing them.

When they were "released" by Brian and sent to the Devorex command ship, the little soldier who had the unique weapon concealed in his tunic, used it on the command staff, pilots, and security. Blue Robe gave the commands to attack the High Scribe's ship and then the others to draw them away from the cave allowing the Hiimori to escape, and Brian to get Jack to the healing pool.

Frank, sitting next to Blue Robe gave the little diplomat a slap on the back, nearly knocking him off the rock he was sitting on, giving him a "well done." Maybe not shooting him had been a good idea. It was possible a kind of friendship was forming.

The soldier also gave some interesting news. Ever since he was dragged into the pool after biting the High Scribe on the leg, he found he didn't have any hunger or desire for the flesh of living creatures. Even the thought was disgusting.

John noted this unexpected development and advised it would need to be explored more fully. Maybe there was hope to make the Devorex a less carnivorous and more peaceful entity in the universe.

Brian talked about Earth's ancient myths and how strange it mirrored everything that had happened, but then he got serious and talked about the new hierarchy of The People.

"With the High Scribe dead, or at least, no longer in power, and the Council nearly decimated, The People will need new leadership. The only member of the Council who is left is Frank, who is the Gun Maker." Turning to Frank, Brian gestured to him. "It appears you have now been elevated to the position of

Guardian of The People."

"Now, wait just a minute," Frank said. "I never said I wanted to be the Guardian of The People. I am the Gun Maker and only the Gun Maker. I have no desire to be anything else on the Council."

"You are the Council," Brian gave a laugh. "You hold every position."

Frank thought about this for a minute. "If I am the Council, and the Council is the final word, then what I declare is the final word, correct?"

"That is as it always has been since the Cleansing," Jack agreed.

"Then that is what we must change. We have lived under a system far less ideal than we were led to believe," Frank started, "and it was allowed to become corrupt. No longer will the few and powerful rule the many or the weak without them having a say in their leaders, their way of life, and their future. No one will dictate how another must live, how they must feel, or who they must follow. There are no perfect systems and we will make mistakes. We will fail in many aspects; however, we will learn, and we will grow, and we will be better for it."

Brian stood and started clapping. Several of the group stared at him, not understanding.

"Now that was a great speech," Brian said. "So, since you only want to be the Gun Maker, I would like to nominate Jack for the position of Guardian of The People."

"That would be fine, however, there is a small problem," Frank stated. "You are not of this world and are not one of The People. By law, you cannot interject anything into The People's governmental process. Therefore, I cannot accept your nomination of Jack."

Brian was astonished.

"That is," Frank continued, "until you are made an official citizen and are declared to be one of The People. We will do this when we get back in the city for all to see and recognize you as one of our greatest heroes."

The others stood and clapped. Even the wind horses were striking their hooves on the ground.

Now, Brian was flabbergasted.

CHAPTER 58

Frank, as the current Guardian of The People, called for a very rare holiday. The People were told of the events involving the High Scribe; his crimes against Sarangerel, the Guardian of The People, and the Council, as well as his plot with the Devorex to rid the planet of all humans. He betrayed The People and his position, and his name was removed from all places it once hung with honor. They were not told of his current fate.

Brian was brought before The People and celebrated as a hero. He was given full citizenship as one of The People and as a token of their friendship and gratitude, he was given a new spaceship all his own. It had a name painted on the sides; "Angie".

The wind horses were recognized as natural citizens, but even more, they were given special protection status. The river valley was officially designated as their rightful land and it was not to be encroached upon without their permission. The secret of the healing pool was not spoken of and was theirs to protect. However, they did allow John to experiment with the Devorex at the pool and there were some very promising results.

Frank also gave notice about another strange occurrence that would be happening soon; elections.

This concept needed to be explained to more than a few of The People. Worthy candidates would need to come forward or be found to fill all the open positions. There were no separate political parties and the platforms were all the same, so picking a candidate was not a simple task."

After the celebrations died down, Frank got Brian alone for a conversation.

"You know there is a place for you on the Council if you want," Frank stated.

"Politics?" Brian quipped. "Not for me on any world."

"I was thinking more of a job in law enforcement," Frank suggested. "We are going to need someone with experience in these matters."

"I don't mind helping get some of The People trained for you, but I think I have retired from active duty. Besides, I hear there are other humans out there in the universe. I'd like to go out there and find them."

"Meet me tomorrow morning at the Angie," Frank said. "I have something to show you."

"Are we going somewhere?"

"You will see. Come alone."

CHAPTER 59

Brian got to the Angie early. He wanted to go over the systems for the new ship. He still had a tingling feeling in his stomach every time he heard the name or saw it on the side of the ship. He wished she could see it.

Frank arrived, admiring the ship as well and greeted Brian.

"Okay, so where are we going?" Brian asked, hand on his hips.

"To my lab on the moon," he said. "There is still much work to do."

"Work on what?" Brian asked. "Weapons?"

"That will come later. You do know how to fly this thing, or do you want me to take over?"

"Strap in and enjoy the ride. We'll be there in just a few minutes." Brian said, getting into the pilot's seat.

"That long, huh? Wake me when we get there. Unless you get lost or need my help."

The Angie backed off from the dock next to the newly repaired Hiimori. It lifted effortlessly into the air and after it gained a little altitude, it powered up and streaked away, shrinking to a pinpoint before disappearing into space.

In less than three minutes, Brian was docking at Frank's masked lab. When Frank unstrapped and stood, he was a little wobbly.

"Sorry about that, Frank," Brian said hiding a chuckle, "I should have slowed down a bit for you. I forgot about your age."

"At my age, I don't need to go any slower. Time will catch up with me too fast."

They entered the outer building hiding the real lab and then through the portal that opened for Frank. The charade he used to hide its location also fooled the Devorex when they came searching.

He made greetings to all his workers who stayed and continued working during his absence. They were happy to see the new, if only temporary, Guardian of The People.

"Follow me," Frank said as he quickly scurried through the lab. Brian had to hurry to catch up. When they got to the other side of the lab, Frank stood before a large door that was to the area John told him was his private work area. No one besides Frank was allowed inside.

Frank opened the door going inside. He held the door open. "Well, don't just stand there, come on in.

Brian went through the doorway and into a large, bright, shiny room. He could hear the humming of machinery in one corner and what sounded like something boiling on one side. He wasn't sure what to expect.

"Not quite like Frankenstein's castle, is it?" Frank asked, a little smile on his small mouth.

"Uh, no. No, it's not," Brian had to admit, a little embarrassed. "But what are you working on here?"

"Time travel."

"Jack said there were scientist working on time travel and there was some limited success. I didn't know he was talking about you."

"He wasn't. No one knows I'm working on this and I've had more than limited success. I've done it."

"You! You've traveled in time? To where? How far?" Brian asked excitedly.

"A few minutes. It was strange. I couldn't believe it the first time. I had to keep checking my instruments."

"A few minutes? That's it?" Brian asked, exasperated. "What good is that?"

"It's a start. I've worked many years on this to get these results. One day it may be a whole lot more, but it is a work in progress. I'll never give up."

Brian let his hopes soar when he first heard those words, only to get crushed as they came falling down on him. He couldn't blame Frank any more than he could blame a clock. The laws of the universe were working against them.

"There is one other thing I have been working on," Frank said hesitantly, "however, it is not something I'm sure you would fully understand and give your approval of if you knew all the things involved."

"I'm not sure what you are talking about, Frank. I think I'm confused."

"Come this way," Frank said, walking over to the side of the lab. He got to a section that appeared to be set up like a big chemistry experiment.

Brian walked over beside a table and saw a box that looked familiar. "Isn't that my...how did that get here?" Brian's tackle box was sitting on the table.

"Jack brought that back with him from Earth. He thought it might be helpful."

"I didn't know you had fish here. I never saw any."

"No, Brian, there are no fish on this moon or on the planet," Frank gave a slight chuckle.

"Okaaay," Brian shook his head and gave a questioning smile. "Now, I'm really sure I'm confused."

Frank went over to the table and picked up a glass vial and handed it to Brian.

Brian looked in the small vial and saw it contained something. It was a beige strip and it had little red hearts on it. It was the band-aid he once put on Angie's finger after she stuck it with a fish hook. A small amount of her blood was on the pad.

CHAPTER 60

"What are you doing with this?" Brian asked, not really sure if he wanted an answer.

"We have the science and the knowledge to use from the band-aid, Angie's blood, what your scientist call DNA. We can make a perfect copy; a replica if you will, of what Angie was."

Brian was shocked. The thoughts that were running, screaming through his brain made him weak and almost pass out. He grabbed the table, setting the vial down before he dropped it. Frank went to him and helped him to a chair. It took a few minutes before Brian could speak. He didn't take his eyes off the vial.

"You can bring Angie back to life? You can do this?"

"Yes. It is really a very simple process. The growth can be stimulated, and she would be fully grown within a few weeks. It would not take much longer to have her at the age at which you knew her. With her DNA from that moment of collection, we can also revive her memories up to a point and you can help with that. Languages, knowledge, and abilities can be added."

"But it will be Angie?"

"It will be a clone of Angie. As I said, a copy. She will look just like her, sound just like her, act just like her, but you will know what happened to your Angie. That won't change."

"Will she know she's a clone?" Brian asked. "Is there any way that she would be able to find out?"

"No, nor will anyone else."

The revelation was still making Brian's head spin. He could have Angie back, but it wouldn't really be Angie, or would it?

"Are there any complications or side effects, changes in personality, her mental ability, lifespan? Anything I need to worry about?"

"The only worry I would have is you. How would you handle this? Now that you have this knowledge, the decision you make, either way, could lay heavy on your shoulders."

"What would you do?" How would you be able to handle it?"

"I understand your dilemma," Frank said. "It was hard for me the first time as well. It's a decision I've made many times. He went to a door and opened it, inside the lab walked a beautiful, human female. "Brian, I'd like you to meet Eve, my wife."

"Hello, Brian. I've heard so much about you," she said out loud, smiling.

"Hello," Brian said, stepping forward to shake her hand.

"Oh, come on now, you can do better than that. We're almost family," She said, opening her arms to give him a big hug.

Brian felt a little embarrassed. Here was a beautiful, young woman he just met, the wife of one of his friends and the mother of another. It was the first time since Angie that he held a woman in his arms. It was strange and nice, all at the same time.

"I hope we get a chance to talk later. I want to know all about your adventures as a detective and how you like our little part of space," she said, still holding onto his arm."

"I'd like that," Brian said.

"For now, sweetheart," Frank said, "we have a lot of work to do and maybe we can get together for dinner."

"Of course, dear," Eve stated, smiling. Turning to Brian, "He is always so busy either here in the lab or somewhere out there," she said, pointing up. "Maybe you can talk him into slowing down a bit for me. Lord knows I've tried."

"I'll see what I can do," Brian gave a snicker.

She gave his arm a squeeze and went back through the door she entered from.

When she had gone, Frank closed the door. "That is Eve," he said. "She is the tenth—no, the eleventh copy of the original. She is the same as the first, the fifth, and the tenth. She will grow old, get sick, and eventually die. And I will still be here. So, instead of being lonely, heartsick, sad, and depressed, I continue to make copies of the original. Am I selfish? Yes. Am I fooling myself? Maybe. Am I wrong? I don't know."

"You've made eleven copies of Eve? How many can you make?"

"As long as I have a supply of the original DNA, I can make as many as I want. I could have a whole warehouse full. However, there have been many periods of time I have not had any copies of Eve at all. Eve number four died of an accident while we were exploring another world. It took me many years before I decided to make another. I told Eve number seven. I sat her down, I explained it all to her, I showed her the science. She had a hard time accepting it. She eventually had a breakdown.

"Well, I think *if* I were to agree to this, it would be only once. I don't think I could handle doing it more than once in my short lifetime. I don't think I would tell her either."

"I have some more news for you, Brian. I think you better sit back down in the chair."

"What is it? Something bad about Angie?"

"John and I conducted several experiments. I had some suspicions, but we have come to the same conclusion."

"What? Do I have some alien disease? Am I dying? Tell me," Brian begged.

"It seems the waters from the pool in the cavern has some unique properties."

"I know this. It healed Jack. I was also healed of my injuries. I was even refreshed of my exhaustion. Our little Devorex friend no longer wants to chomp on my leg."

"These are wonderful things, things that are good. But I'm not sure if you will understand or welcome what I am about to say."

"You're starting to scare me, Frank. Just get it out, tell me."

"We believe the healing waters have also given you an expanded life cycle."

"You mean I'm going to live for what—a hundred, maybe two hundred years?"

"We don't know how long, but we believe it will be very substantial. Maybe as long as we live."

"But you live for thousands of years. Eons. I don't want to live forever. My body will give out way before that."

"You should not notice any real change in appearance or physical ability. It might be necessary for you to get back to the pool at some point to continue the process just as we must rejuvenate through the spires."

"So, If I wanted to have Angie, or rather, a copy of Angie as a companion, I would see her age and die before I got old. And this could happen over and over. But what about what happened to me. Couldn't the healing pool help both Eve and Angie?"

"No, my friend," Frank said, putting his hand on Brian's shoulder. "We did experiments, checked our results over and over, tried different ways, but it seems the cloning process somehow cancels the effects of the healing waters."

"So, I'll need to decide to clone or not to clone."

It is a conundrum only you will be able to find an answer to. I hope it will be one you can live with all of your long life."

Brian was rocked by the sheer magnitude of all this information. He didn't know what to ask next, but there really didn't seem to be any other remarkable questions needing to have mind shattering answers right at the moment.

That evening, Brian enjoyed a wonderful dinner cooked by Eve that reminded him of Earth. She had insisted that there would be no talk about science, guns, or politics while they were at the table.

Frank almost slipped when he brought up Jack's nomination to head the Council as Guardian of The People, but Eve gave him a look that stopped him in his tracks.

After dinner and saying his farewells, Brian returned to the planet alone. He told Frank he had a lot of thinking to do before deciding about Angie.

Brian went to the spot on the cliffs overlooking the home of the wind horses, remembering his first time there and his amazement at seeing the flying horses as they frolicked in and out of the honey-colored waterfalls.

He thought long about everything that had happened; about Sarangerel, Jack, the High Scribe, the Devorex, and of course, Angie.

He thought about Earth and what it was really like at this time. If he would ever see it again, in the old way or in the future. He didn't try to stop the tears from falling down his face.

The dark stallion met with him and flew him to his home to see the mare and colt. They were both excited to see him. The colt, his little nubby wings fluttering, came right up to him and nudged him with his nose. Brian scratched him behind the ears. Brian was welcome to come anytime.

Brian returned to the spaceship dock and over the next few days did some work on his ship. He added an extra stasis pod and a custom chair at the command console.

Brian had decided to go exploring and see if he could find other humans or new worlds and any other interesting creatures. He would leave in the next day or so.

John was working on the new government for The People and getting elections set up. He had help from an experienced diplomat; Blue Robe, now known by his new name, George. George found a new indulgent. He discovered he was very fond of the strange fruit that was served to the humans.

There was an influx of humans as stasis pods were opened. The humans from so many Earth time periods and cultures created a whole new problem for John. Jack had accepted the nomination for Guardian of The People and it looked like no one else wanted the job. The job of Gun Maker was sure to go to Frank. There was no one else more qualified nor who wanted to get blown up.

Brian had the hardest time saying goodbye to Jack. He was Brian's scarecrow even though he had a brain. They were like brothers now. Brian insisted he would be back one day soon, but Jack was afraid he wouldn't return.

Jack said he would forget being Guardian of The People and volunteered to go with Brian, but Brian already had a traveling companion and The People needed Jack. The week before he left, he and Jack were inseparable.

A farewell festivity was held the night before Brian's departure and goodbyes were said over and over. Many attempts were made to try and talk him out of going, but his mind was set.

Later that night, he went to Sarangerel's. He went to tell her goodbye and to thank her.

The following morning, Brian took a disk out to the falls to see the wind horses one more time. He was especially happy to see the young colt getting strong. He visioned him flying over the river one day, big and powerful wings just like his father. He gave both the dark stallion and the mare, a hug, wishing them well. The mare even had a tear running down her face.

Later that morning, Brian had everything ready to leave and a large group of disks escorted him to his ship. Few words were exchanged at the dock. Emotions were running high with everyone.

Without too much hesitation, he went up the ramp,

stopping at the open door. Brain took his fedora off his head and waved it to all his friends who were gathered to send him off. He put the hat back on and gave a salute then patted his chest over his heart. Stepping inside, he closed the hatch on the Angie.

Brian blinked a tear away and cleared his throat. "Take her out," he told his co-pilot.

The sleek ship lifted slowly from the dock, but Brian had not told his co-pilot what direction to head.

"Let's try that way, Ringo," Brian said to his newly named friend, pointing to a place in the sky.

A series of agreeable clicks from the little Devorex sitting at the controls filled the air and then a very raspy, slithery voice spoke. "Yes sir, Captain."

The Angie left the planet, heading into space to search for other humans and a way to return Brian to the world he knew and maybe, just maybe, even his wife. Now that would be justice.

The End

Maybe

Thank you so much for reading my breakout science fiction novel, "No Space For Justice". I hope you enjoyed it.

Please check out my other works listed in the front of the book (Listed under 'Books You Really Need to Buy') and keep your eye out for other exciting stories and adventures coming your way soon.

Again, thank you,

William N. Gilmore

About the Author

William N. Gilmore is an honorably discharged Vietnam era veteran (1972 to 1978) of the U. S. Army. He served as a Military Policeman in the U. S. at numerous posts, including four years at Fort McPherson, GA and in Gelnhausen, Germany. Upon discharge, he stayed in the Atlanta area.

From 1979 to 1981 he was an Assistant Security Chief at the Omni International Hotel and Entertainment complex in downtown Atlanta.

In January 1981 he joined the Atlanta Police Department, working the streets as a patrolman until he was promoted to detective. His next fifteen years were spent as a detective with the Narcotics Squad. William retired with nearly twenty-seven years on the force.

Shortly before retiring, he began writing again, this time with his main characters as people he could relate with; Atlanta Police Detectives.

William has several other books available including a three-book detective series:

Book One: *Blue Bloods & Black Hearts*
Book Two: *Gold Badges & Dark Souls*
Book Three: *Blue Knights & White Lies*

He also has the first book out in a new series that is a

very historical, paranormal, detective story:

Caution in the Wind - Book One: Partnerships

Caution in the Wind - Book Two: The Treasure Seekers
Coming Soon

All of William's books are works of fiction (wink-wink) and are available at Amazon Books and if you are lucky enough to live in Georgia, and near Hiram, at the Hiram Bookstore.

William is a proud member of the Paulding County Writers' Guild in Hiram, GA where he lives with his wife Esther.

He likes veterans and active duty military, police and other first responders, writing, playing poker, metal detecting, telling stupid jokes, history, science, space, investigations into the unknown, UFO's, and aliens, the Braves, the Falcons, and eating. Not all in that order.

About the Cover Artist

Alex Storer is an artist, musician and graphic designer based in Derbyshire, UK.

A lifelong interest in science fiction came full circle in 2010, when Alex finally began realising his own visions of future times and places. Taking inspiration from classic SF literature and the SF&F art greats of the 1970s and 80s, his work pays homage to yesterday's visions of tomorrow, yet remains contemporary and distinctive in style.

Alex first encountered computer art during a school art class in 1990 – a moment that would ultimately define his career as a graphic designer and digital artist. Today he enjoys creative collaborations with independent authors and publishers, and regularly exhibits his artwork on the UK science fiction convention scene.

Alex's H.G. Wells-inspired painting *Awakening* was included in *Brave New Worlds: Utopias/Dystopias* in London in 2011, and his work has previously appeared *in ImagineFX Magazine, Computer Arts, Writing and Illustrating the Graphic Novel* (Mike Chinn) and *How to Draw and Sell Comics* (Alan McKenzie). In 2017, Alex was commissioned to produce a unique piece of artwork (albeit a non-science fiction one) that was presented to HRH Prince William The Duke of Cambridge.

Also a musician, Alex has been composing atmospheric instrumental music since 2006 under the name The Light Dreams. It comes as no surprise that there is an overlap between Alex's art and music, which takes influence from classic science fiction novels and artists such as Jean-Michel Jarre and Mike Oldfield.

In 2012, he was invited to be an honorary musician and artist for the Initiative for Interstellar Studies (i4is.org) and has since released several albums in support of the Initiative. Alex continues to independently produce and publish his music online via the Bandcamp platform.

Websites:
http://www.thelightdream.net
http://thelightdreams.bandcamp.com

Email: alex@thelightdream.net

Made in the USA
Columbia, SC
10 November 2018